GIRL GANG

BOOK 1

The Journey Continues

KATRINA KAHLER

KC Global Enterprises Pty Ltd

Table of Contents

Reader's Note

Dear Reader,

Girl Gang is the continuation of our bestselling series, Twins and The New Girl. We have received endless requests for these series to continue, so we decided to make this happen.
Girl Gang is the ongoing story of all the main characters. As the series unfolds, new characters will appear with even more drama and excitement unfolding.

We hope you enjoy Girl Gang just as much as the two series before it. If you haven't read Twins or The New Girl yet, you'll find them on Amazon or your favorite online bookstore.

Thank you so much for reading our books and for your continued support.

Wishing you the very best,
Katrina and Kaz xx

PROLOGUE

(Final Chapter of The New Girl – Book 15)

Alexa

I sat in the courtyard with my friends, listening to another funny Elijah joke. I'd often wondered if he searched the internet for jokes because he seemed to have an endless supply. Damon was seated beside me, his warm laughter filling my ears. When his arm brushed against mine, our eyes connected, and a welcome spark trickled delightfully up my spine.

Our weekly triathlon training sessions had brought us even closer. And thanks to Damon's coaching in the pool plus some training from Casey, I'd improved my stroke. There were still a couple of weeks before the competition day, and with extra pool sessions planned, I hoped to improve even further.

Content and at peace with the world, I sat back and surveyed our group. Elijah continued to flirt with Cora while she giggled happily beside him. On the weekend, they'd gone to the cinema together. Even though both their younger sisters had tagged along, we were all calling it their first official date. During a girls-only sleepover at the twins' house, which was so much fun I hadn't wanted it to end, Cora kept insisting that her date with Elijah wasn't an actual date; they were just hanging out. We refused to believe her and decided it would only be a matter of time, and the pair would become a real couple.

Cora had prodded me about Damon, suggesting that we would be the next to date. Casey and Brie were also convinced it was bound to happen. So far, though, Damon and I remained close friends, and although there was a spark between us, I sensed him keeping a friendly distance which I was grateful for. I'd been through so much and was content to take things slowly. Like Ali and Lucy, I wasn't yet ready for a boyfriend. We were only thirteen, after all. There was plenty of time ahead of us for more serious relationships with boys.

Now that Ali, Mike, and Sai were the best of friends, we all blended like a big happy family that warmed my heart. I wanted our group to stay friends forever, and I hoped it would be the case. Already, we were discussing plans for the summer ahead. I knew it would be the most wonderful summer ever.

The best part of all was that after Meg's suspension, she didn't return to school. Instead, she messaged Ali with the excuse that her grandmother was ill and needed to be cared for, so she and her mom were forced to leave town. Meg also confided that she'd be returning to her old school. She ended her text by apologizing to Ali for taking her things, claiming it was just a fun prank and she meant nothing by it. She then asked Ali to stay in touch. Ali scoffed at this. She never wanted to speak to Meg again.

Whether Meg was telling the truth about her grandmother, we didn't know. But the news had shocked us to our core. Meg's short stay had caused endless chaos, and then she'd disappeared from our lives just as suddenly as she had appeared in the first place. As Ali said, hopefully, this time, she stayed away forever.

My eyes drifted across the courtyard to where Holly sat alongside Ronnie. Since Meg's departure, Ronnie and Holly had made amends. According to Sammi, Ronnie had offered Holly a massive apology and come crawling back. How Sammi knew so much gossip was a mystery to me, but she could always be relied on to share one story or another.

Neither Ronnie nor Holly had other friends to turn to, and it seemed inevitable that they'd eventually reform their bond, especially without Meg around to create a rift between them. Without Meg's presence, Ronnie was also a meeker, milder version of her former self. Perhaps the embarrassment of being suspended had finally put her in her place. Knowing Ronnie, though, she'd probably bounce back at some point. Next time, I planned to be ready for her.

With Meg gone from our lives, I felt as though a huge burden had been lifted from my shoulders, and everything settled into a beautiful rhythm.

Tyler was yet to spend a weekend with our mother, who had so far been 'too busy' for him to stay over. Uncle Vern had filled his spare time with fun outings that Tyler adored. I sensed that our uncle enjoyed spending time with Tyler just as much.

Aunt Beth kept telling my brother and me that we had the world at our feet, and we should embrace every opportunity. I planned to do precisely that, and every day, I counted my blessings for the miracles that had come to pass.

"You look deep in thought." Damon broke through my

reverie with a nudge of his shoulder against mine.

I brushed at my hair and smiled. "I was just thinking about how lucky I am to have such a great group of friends."

When his mouth curved into a beautiful Damon grin, my happiness bubbled over.

CHAPTER ONE

Ali

I chewed on a hangnail as I surveyed the bush track behind us for the third time. Overhanging shrubs rustled in the afternoon breeze, heightening the eeriness of the scene. Students were perched on rocks, boulders, or the dusty ground, weary from the mountain hike and the hot sun still beating down. It had been a tiring but fun end-of-semester field trip for our grade, one of the many activities organized to celebrate our final days of middle school. Everyone was now ready to head home, and several kids were asking the teachers if we could board the bus. However, with two students missing, Ms. Harris said we weren't going anywhere. When

Mr. Henriksen, the other supervising teacher, finally exited the trail, everyone turned hopefully in his direction.

He regarded Ms. Harris with a shake of his head, indicating that Ronnie and Holly hadn't been found. "I went all the way back to Pike's Ridge, but no luck. They must have taken a wrong turn. They could be anywhere by now."

Our teacher's face sagged, the worry lines creasing her brow and forehead as she and Mr. Henriksen carried on a whispered conversation. A wrenching fear gripped my insides. If Ronnie and Holly were lost, it was all my fault. I was the one who'd pointed them along a different trail...a split-second decision that I desperately wished I could take back.

"We should have gone after them," Casey muttered worriedly.

Sammi Brownstone's head swiveled toward us. As always, her supersonic hearing was in full force. "Do you know where they went?"

I shrugged my shoulders, silently cursing her for eavesdropping. Sammi had an uncanny sixth sense for gossip, and if there was ever any circulating, she was always within earshot. Her eyes flicked questioningly between Casey and me. We slid across the rock and lowered our voices so she could no longer hear us.

"You need to tell Mr. Henriksen which track the girls took," Casey murmured, keeping her voice low. "If they don't find their way down, they could be stuck on the mountain all night."

I gulped anxiously. Casey was right; I had no choice. Getting reluctantly to my feet, I approached the teachers. "Excuse me, Ms. Harris, Mr. Henriksen...I um, I saw Ronnie and Holly take a detour."

Our teacher's brow furrowed, and I noted the stress that filled her features. "A detour?"

I sucked in a breath and nodded. "There was a fork in the trail. I think they might have gone right instead of left."

10

"Why didn't you stop them? And why didn't you tell me this before?"

"I, uh, I thought the trails linked up. That's what the sign said. The girls should've ended up back on the main trail, and I didn't think it would be a problem."

"That must be Captain's Loop," Mr. Henriksen mused. "But it actually branches off in two different directions. One branch returns to the main trail, but the other traverses the mountain and leads down the opposite side."

Ms. Harris turned back to me, and I sensed her frustration. "Ali, I don't understand why you didn't tell me this sooner."

"I was expecting them to show up. I didn't know the trail went elsewhere."

She shook her head, confused. None of what I was saying made sense. She knew it, and I did too. But if I admitted the truth, I'd be in terrible trouble.

"Go and sit down," she snapped. "And if you suddenly remember anything else, please let me know!"

I returned to my spot next to Casey and watched Ms. Harris unclip the walkie-talkie from her belt. We had limited phone reception at the base of the mountain, but it was nonexistent on the trails. The teachers had been relying on walkie-talkies to contact each other during the hike. We heard her speak to Mr. Ridgway, the support teacher who'd accompanied us and who was still searching for the girls. Ms. Harris recounted what I'd just told her, and Mr. Ridgway's crackly voice responded, saying he'd already checked the Captain's Loop trails with no luck.

When I heard a yelp from across the way, I whipped my head around to see Austin Hannigan from our class throwing gravel at a group of boys sitting nearby.

"Austin!" Ms. Harris screeched. "Stop that right now!"

"Josh and Miles started it! They threw rocks at me first!" Austin hollered back.

"Josh and Miles. Move over here and sit by me. Now!"

Our teacher's patience had worn thin but so had the patience of all the students. Various groups were growing restless and making nuisances of themselves. While Ms. Harris tried to settle them down, Mr. Henriksen tapped at his phone screen. I heard him ask to speak with Mrs. Jensen. He then walked away, and his voice faded.

Casey's fearful gaze turned back to me. "Imagine if Mr. Ridgway can't find them. Imagine if Ronnie and Holly end up stuck here overnight."

"Casey, please don't say that. Mr. Ridgway knows the trails better than anyone. Of course, he'll find them." I dug my toe into the dirt under my feet. It wasn't like my twin to be so negative, and her reaction was causing my anxiety to soar. If I hadn't been so reckless, none of us would be in this dilemma now. But when the opportunity arose to trick the girls, my words had popped out of their own accord. And once I said them, I couldn't take them back.

I recalled reaching the fork in the trail. My shoelace had come undone, so I stopped to tie it. I then paused for a drink from my water bottle. I wasn't in shape like the others, and they'd all raced ahead. Behind me, I could hear the distant voices of Mr. Ridgway and his group of kids trailing us. They'd taken up the rear and set a slow pace.

Meanwhile, Ronnie and Holly had been on my tail for the entire climb, and when they turned the bend and came into view, Hollie's smug expression caused my irritation to spike. Ever since she'd been asked to perform with Mike at our graduation ceremony as well as sing the lead in the band, she hadn't stopped boasting. I understood she was excited, but she didn't need to brag.

Ronnie's comments had aggravated me further. It seemed that every time I was within earshot, she was blabbing about Holly's upcoming performance. When the pair stopped to ponder the two trails branching in different directions, I realized they hadn't noticed the sign. Admittedly, it was partly covered by an overhanging tree branch, but instead of pointing out the map I'd already perused myself, I decided to trick them.

"It's that way." I indicated the track on the right. "You guys go ahead; I'm just taking a rest."

Without giving the matter any more thought, they followed my directions and traipsed ahead. Laughter bubbled in my throat as I watched them disappear around a bend.

I hurried along the other trail and saw Casey walking toward me. "There you are!" she called out. "I thought you must've got lost."

"I just sent Ronnie and Holly along the other track," I snickered in amusement.

"But everyone's gone this way." Casey pointed behind her.

"Don't worry. I checked the sign. The trail they took loops back onto the main one about a mile further on. A bit of extra walking won't hurt them. Plus, they deserve it."

Casey looked behind me, but the girls were nowhere in sight. I tugged on her t-shirt. "Come on, let's catch up to the others." I then ran on ahead.

When Casey called out to Holly, I let out a frustrated sigh. She was ruining my prank. But there was no response, so she gave up and followed behind me. Now I was paying the price. What I'd thought was a harmless joke had become serious, and I was helpless to do anything about it.

My stomach sank even lower when Ms. Harris suddenly announced that we were heading back to school.

"When I say your name, please board the bus!" she yelled as she took her clipboard from her backpack and started checking people's names off her list.

Sammi stepped forward. "What about Ronnie and Holly? We can't leave them behind."

"Mr. Ridgway is looking for them," Ms. Harris replied. "Please get on the bus, Sammi."

"But how will they get home?" Sammi countered. "And what if Mr. Ridgway can't find them?"

13

Miss Harris frowned irritably. "Mrs. Jensen is on her way here. Now stop worrying. Mr. Ridgway will find the girls, and Mrs. Jensen will drive them all back to school. Enough questions, just get on the bus."

I darted an uncomfortable glance at Casey. What was supposed to have been a minor prank had turned into a disaster, and I was to blame. There would be questions asked, but that wasn't what worried me most. What if Sammi and Casey were right? What if the girls weren't found? I'd heard of hikers getting lost on trails and spending days in the wilderness. What if that happened to Ronnie and Holly?

The day that had begun as a fun end-of-semester field trip for our grade had become a nightmare.

And Ali Jackson, school captain, was to blame.

CHAPTER TWO

Casey

I chose a seat beside my twin, who was staring aimlessly out the bus window. Her anxiety caused my own nervous thoughts to escalate. When Ali said she'd sent Ronnie and Holly along the wrong trail, my instincts had warned me against the idea. If only I'd taken notice and chased after the two girls.

Alexa and Damon sat behind us, the pair oblivious to what had taken place. Brie sat with Lucy while Cora was engrossed in Elijah beside her. Jake turned to look at me from his spot next to Mike. I offered him a half-hearted smile. Not even he knew the truth. No one knew except Ali and me. While the debacle had been Ali's doing, I also felt responsible.

Sammi's gossiping from the seat in front of us filled my ears. "If Mr. Ridgway doesn't find them, they'll freeze on the mountain overnight," she ranted to the girl beside her. "They'll have no food and water. They could die up there."

She was making the situation so much worse, and I wished she'd stop. But she wasn't the only one. Everyone was talking about the missing girls, and a subdued atmosphere filled the bus.

"Don't worry," I muttered in Ali's ear in an effort to be positive. "Mr. Ridgway knows the trails. He said he's hiked all over that mountain heaps of times. He'll find them."

Ali's eyes slipped to mine, and she nodded. But I was aware of her doubts. I felt them too. I laid my head back on the headrest and closed my eyes. Why had Holly felt the need to brag? Everyone already knew she had the best voice of all the singers. It wasn't necessary to boast. As for Ronnie, I suspected she was trying to support Holly in any way she could. After the saga with Meg, we'd all thought her friendship with Holly was doomed. But Ronnie managed to worm back into Holly's life, and the pair had been inseparable ever since.

"You'll be the star of the grad ceremony, Holly," Ronnie had insisted, raising her voice so that Ali heard every word. "*And*, you and Mike should definitely busk during the summer. You'll make heaps of money."

"We've talked about it. Mike's keen, so we probably will," Holly replied cheerily.

It was at this point that my twin whipped around. I sent her a warning look, hoping she'd keep her retort to herself. I urged her to keep walking. Unfortunately, she lagged behind our group, and the rest was history.

When the sound of Alexa's laughter met my ears, I peeked over the back of my seat and saw Damon whispering in her ear as he spun Alexa's bracelet around her wrist. Since the triathlon, they'd truly bonded. Although Alexa kept saying she wasn't ready for a boyfriend, they'd probably be united before long.

The triathlon itself seemed a lifetime ago, especially with that day's dramas taking precedence in my head. I recalled the moment I crossed the triathlon finish line, so exhausted I was ready to collapse. Alexa, who had fallen behind in the swim leg, had made excellent time in the cycling and run sections and ended up reaching the finish line just after me. Damon managed second place, beating everyone in our group. But we all made the top twenty which was an incredible achievement. Thankfully, this year, none of us was injured.

Surrounded by the turmoil of the field trip, the triathlon felt like a dream. Crossing my fingers, I prayed that Mr. Ridgway would call to say Holly and Ronnie had been found.

Unfortunately, when we arrived back at school, we were met with the worried face of Mrs. Watkins, the assistant principal.

"Any news?" Ms. Harris asked.

Mrs. Watkins shook her head.

CHAPTER THREE

Holly

I tugged my phone from my pocket for the umpteenth time. Once again, the words, 'No Service,' stared back. Sighing heavily, I checked my surroundings. "I think I recognize that huge tree. Didn't we pass it a little while back? I feel like we're going around in circles, Ronnie. Maybe we should stay here and wait for someone to find us."

Ronnie threw her arms in the air in disgust. "This sucks so badly. How did this happen?"

"Because I let you take over. I knew we were going the wrong way. Why don't you ever listen to me?"

"So, it's my fault?" Ronnie scowled.

Frustrated and exhausted, I heaved out another sigh. I

had wanted to turn back, but she insisted we keep walking. By the time we eventually backtracked, we couldn't find the junction we needed. It was as though it no longer existed.

"It doesn't make sense," Ronnie griped. "Ali was right behind us. Mr. Ridgway was trailing us with a few other kids as well. How did we lose them all?"

I shrugged my shoulders, angry that I'd allowed Ronnie to take charge. When would I ever learn?

I still hadn't forgiven her for ditching me for Meg, and now we were fighting again. Admittedly, after Meg left town, Ronnie had apologized repeatedly for the way she treated me. She even begged me to forgive her, anything so I'd be her friend again. It felt good to see her crawl. After the way she'd treated me, she still had a lot of making up to do.

But now we were in a terrible mess. The further we walked, the thicker the bush became. The sun was also sinking lower in the sky. "It's getting late, Ronnie. What if we're stranded up here overnight?"

Ronnie's eyes slid worriedly to mine. I knew she was thinking the same thing. I watched her cup her hands around her mouth. "Hello! Is anyone there? Ms. Harris? Mr. Henriksen? Anybody?"

Her voice was hoarse from yelling. Mine felt the same way. We'd been calling and calling. Why hadn't someone come looking for us?

"Let's go this way," Ronnie indicated the track on her left. "It looks like it leads down the mountain. We need to reach the bottom before dark. Hopefully, we'll get cell service and can call someone to collect us."

"Should we stay where we are? Wait for them to find us?"

"Look at the sun, Holly. Not a lot of daylight left. I don't want to be stuck on this mountain in the dark, do you?"

I stumbled after her, holding my phone in the air as I tried to get a connection, my fear escalating with every step.

19

CHAPTER FOUR

Ronnie

I was just as scared as Holly, my fear of being lost in the wilderness gripping every part of my core and turning it to mush. I recalled Ali standing at the fork in the trail. Had she followed us, or had we taken the wrong track? My head was a mass of confusion, and I couldn't be sure.

Holly walked silently behind me, and all I could hear was the crackling of the undergrowth beneath our shoes. The dense trees and shrubs mocked us as we passed. I trudged relentlessly on, determined to find a way down the mountain and cell service so we could phone for help. At the very least, we needed to find a house or a road and hopefully a passing car — someone to rescue us. There was no other alternative.

As I walked, I thought back over the events of the previous weeks. When Meg's face came to mind, my stomach clenched into an even tighter knot. If she saw the dilemma I was currently in, she'd probably laugh in my face. I felt like slapping her and wished that I could. The way she'd blamed me for taking Ali Jackson's things was beyond belief. Something I still hadn't come to terms with. How could she do that when the idea had been hers all along?

I'd hurled a couple of abusive texts her way before deciding to block her from all my social media accounts. It was a huge relief to learn she'd returned to her old school, but it hadn't helped my situation at home.

My dad was still freaking out over the whole fiasco. He was even threatening to ban me from the end-of-year dance. Many middle schools in our region didn't hold a junior prom, which made our event extra special. It was all everyone could talk about. And now, because of Meg's influence, I was at risk of missing out. I could also be grounded for half the summer. The entire scenario with the girl I'd thought was my friend hung over me like a dark cloud.

In the midst of it all was a question that still hadn't been answered. I was reluctant to confront Holly, but the issue continued to play on my mind.

"I can't believe we're lost," Holly moaned from behind me. "I told you we should take the other track, Ronnie. You never listen to me."

I whirled on her. "So you *are* blaming me?"

"It was your idea to veer right instead of left."

Pausing mid-step, I glared, unable to keep my frustrations to myself. "You told on us, didn't you?"

"What are you talking about?"

"You told Mrs. Jensen that Meg and I took Ali's things. It was you, wasn't it?"

She blanched. "Why are you bringing that up now?"

"Because…I just need to know."

21

With a shake of her head, she tried to storm past me. "We haven't got time for this, Ronnie. We need to keep walking."

I pulled on her arm, forcing her to stop. "I'm not moving until you tell me the truth. Did you tell Mrs. Jensen that Meg and I were responsible? I know you overheard us talking in the library that day. It had to be you."

I watched her draw in a breath. She probably thought I'd put the issue behind me. Riddled with guilt over the way I'd treated her, I had intended to do just that. I also wanted our friendship to return to the way it was, so I'd remained silent. But it had been eating away at me, and even though I thought I knew the answer, I wanted Holly to admit the truth.

"Yes, I told her. And you deserved it," she scoffed, ripping her arm away. "You were blaming Alexa for things she didn't do. You set her up, and it wasn't fair."

"But she pranked me with Damon's phone," I argued. "It was my way of getting back at her."

"She didn't deserve to be set up by you and Meg. That was cruel."

Holly was taking Alexa's side, and I couldn't understand why. "You got me into so much trouble, Holly. Why would you do that?"

"You weren't exactly my friend at the time, were you?" she spat back. "Or have you conveniently forgotten that detail?"

She marched past me, her shoulders tight. I snorted in disgust and trekked after her.

Deep down, I understood how she felt. I'd been a terrible friend and could hardly blame her for lashing out by telling on me. I suddenly regretted mentioning the incident. If I weren't careful, she'd push me away, and I'd be forced back to my loner status in the library during lunch breaks. It wasn't the way I wanted to end my final two weeks of middle school. Then there was the summer ahead. Surely my father would unground me for that. Holly and I had already made plans,

22

and I didn't want to jeopardize the fun ahead for us. If we ever got off the mountain, that was.

Returning my thoughts to the problem at hand, I pushed forward, fully aware that the sun had sunk even lower. With the temperature growing cooler, I pulled a sweater from my backpack, glad that I'd thought to bring one. Hopefully, Holly had too. There may only be minimal daylight left, and we needed to find a way home before it grew dark. Finding ourselves stranded overnight was too distressing a thought even to contemplate.

CHAPTER FIVE

Ali

Later that afternoon, Casey and I were still waiting anxiously for news that Ronnie and Holly had been found. Our phones vibrated with Instagram DMs that were keeping us in the loop. We'd set up a group chat that included everyone from our group at school…the girls and the boys. Elijah had learned that an official rescue team had mounted a search, confirming my worst fears. The girls were hopelessly lost, and so far, no one had found them. All because of my spontaneous decision to send them along a different trail.

"What if gets dark and they're still not found?" Casey asked. "People die in the wilderness all the time, Ali. What if…"

"Casey, you're not helping!" The negative version of

my sister kept rearing her head. It was one I didn't see very often, but Casey was struggling to spin her thoughts around.

"But if they die up there, it'll be our fault. We could be charged with murder."

I shot her a dark look. "They're not going to die! The rescue people are experienced. They'll know where to look. And Casey, you're not responsible for this. I am."

As she held my gaze, I noticed the frantic throb of her pulse at the base of her neck. "I should have tried harder to call them back," she groaned. "I should've gone after them."

I shook my head. It wasn't right for her to feel guilty. "I did this, Casey. Not you."

When we heard our mother calling us to set the table for dinner, I blew out a reluctant breath and got to my feet. Casey followed me downstairs to the kitchen, where a newsreader's voice sounded from the TV mounted to the wall. It was our parents' habit to listen to the news while they prepared dinner, and as I paused to listen, my anxiety surged to even greater heights.

"Two thirteen-year-old girls from Somerton Middle School have been reported missing while on a school-based hike up Mount Banks this afternoon," the newsreader announced. "When the rest of the group returned to the base, it was discovered that the girls weren't amongst them. One of the teachers, an experienced hiker familiar with the mountain trails, mounted a thorough search with no luck. A rescue team has spent the last hour scouring the area, but there is still no sign of the two teens. A helicopter search is now underway, though there is limited daylight remaining."

Mom turned to us in alarm. "She's talking about your field trip! What's going on? Who's missing?"

My eyes darted to Casey. Neither of us had been willing to share the news. But our parents were bound to find out at some point.

"Ronnie Miller and Holly Neumann," Casey said in response to our mother's question.

25

"Those poor girls!" Dad exclaimed. "They must be terrified."

"And their poor parents," Mom added. "I can't imagine what they're going through right now."

A mountain of guilt welled inside me as I opened the cutlery drawer and counted out five sets of knives and forks. If only I could turn back the clock. When I later sat down at the dining table, not even my father's infamous chicken casserole could tempt me, and I picked at the serving on my plate.

"Not hungry tonight, Ali?" Dad asked from across the table.

I forced a forkful of chicken into my mouth and shrugged as visions of Ronnie and Holly cowering under a tree somewhere in the dark while trying desperately to stay warm haunted my thoughts.

On endless occasions in the past, Casey and I had wanted to wreak havoc on Ronnie, any form of payback we could think of for her bullying and the way she'd taunted Alexa and us. When Holly joined the school band and started chasing after Mike, she was added to my list of most hated people. As much as I'd wanted to make them both suffer, I would never intentionally plan something so dire.

While the drama had been unintended, I was still at fault, and the guilt sat heavily in the pit of my stomach. The damage had been done, and now all I could do was hope for the best.

CHAPTER SIX

Alexa

On the school bus the next morning, the twins were unusually quiet. Even though they despised Ronnie and Holly, they were still worried. I felt the same way. Our group chat line was rife with descriptions of various scenarios where lost hikers were never seen again. Ronnie and Holly were two young girls on their own. Even if they did find their way back down the mountain, it didn't mean they were safe. If a random stranger picked them up, they could end up in even more trouble.

Overnight exposure was another huge concern. Although it was almost summer, the mountain temperatures were still very cold. We'd each taken a backpack on the hike, filled with lunch, snacks, and water. We'd also been instructed to take a sweater and a raincoat in case the weather changed. I pictured the shorts and t-shirts the girls had been wearing and hoped they'd packed something warm, though a shortage of food and water would add to their list of problems.

When we arrived at school, Casey led us onto a grassy verge away from other kids to wait for Brie. She glanced tentatively around her then locked her eyes on mine. "There's something Ali and I haven't told you."

My gaze swung to Ali. "What is it?" I pressed. "What's wrong?"

Ali looked at her twin and nodded. Casey sighed heavily then her words tumbled out. "It's our fault that Ronnie and Holly are missing."

"No, it's *my* fault," Ali countered. "*I'm* to blame."

Her grim expression spoke volumes, and I gulped uneasily. "What do you mean?"

"I told Ronnie and Holly to take a detour," Ali explained, her voice shaky.

"A detour? What detour?" Brie interrupted as she stepped up beside us.

Ali's gaze slid worriedly to Brie. "There was a fork in the trail. I was on my own with Ronnie and Holly, and I pretended everyone had taken the right fork when they really went left. The girls went right and didn't realize I wasn't behind them. They should have linked back up with us, but they never showed up."

Brie frowned. She was just as confused as me. "Why did you do that?"

"They kept bragging about Holly's performance at the grad assembly!" Ali huffed as she tried to explain herself. "You do know Mr. Flynn decided Holly should sing the lead in the band? As well as performing in the duo with Mike? She and Ronnie kept going on and on about it. And…well, I guess I reacted." Ali seemed to realize how petty it all sounded, and her shoulders drooped. "It was all so spontaneous. I was sick of their boasting and wanted to make them walk further than the rest of us. Suffer a little bit. I checked the map. Their track should have looped back onto ours...it was supposed to be a harmless prank."

The cycle of revenge had continued, but rather than an innocent prank, it had caused two girls' lives to be at risk. Not even Ronnie and Holly deserved that. I was about to respond when I saw the color drain from Ali's face. I whipped my head around to see what had caught her attention. Behind us was Sammi Brownstone. Instantly, I knew...she'd heard every word Ali had said.

"OMG, Ali!" Sammi blurted out. "How could you do that? If those girls die, it'll be all your fault!"

I lifted my hand, hoping to restrain Sammi, to warn her to keep the news to herself. But it was too late. She was already racing away from us and into the building. I had no doubt, the gossip train would soon be in full swing, and Ali would be found out.

Ali's eyes darted wildly to Casey, then to Brie and me. Of course, the primary concern was for the lost girls to be found. But if Ali had intentionally directed them onto an alternate trail, she'd be made to pay. I knew it, Brie knew it, and so did both the twins.

When we entered the classroom, Sammi's gaze tracked Ali to her desk. No one else seemed to take any notice, and I wondered if for once, Sammi had kept the latest gossip to herself.

Ms. Harris looked pale and drawn, and there were dark circles under her eyes, as though she hadn't slept. I sensed that she was concerned about the missing girls, but she didn't acknowledge Ali at all. Clearly, Sammi hadn't shared her news with the teacher. I began to hope that she might keep quiet after all.

After everyone had trickled into the room and Ms. Harris was preparing to call attendance, Mr. Ridgway appeared in the doorway. Ms. Harris gave him a questioning look, and he nodded his head, a broad smile crossing his face. "I've just heard…Ronnie and Holly were found a short while ago. They're both okay. They've been taken to the hospital to be checked, but apparently, they'll be fine."

The classroom erupted into a loud whoop, and I turned around in my seat to face Ali. Clutching two overlapped hands to her chest, she threw her head back in relief. My gaze was then drawn to Sammi, who was looking our way. Her eyebrows lifted as she slowly shook her head. I wondered if it was a warning of sorts, a possible threat.

Would she eventually spread the details she'd heard? And would Ronnie and Holly learn the truth?

If that happened, what then?

CHAPTER SEVEN

Ronnie

Holly and I had stumbled along a trail at the base of the mountain, desperately trying to get service on our phones. When I looked up to see two people walking toward us, my relief washed over me in waves. It seemed too good to be true, a miracle of such monumental proportions that I struggled to believe my eyes. When we learned the men were part of a rescue team who'd been sent to search for us, Holly started to cry. Tears spilled from my eyes too.

The men offered to take our backpacks then gave us each a drink of water, which we accepted gratefully. I poured the soothing liquid greedily down my throat, thankful for the granola bar that was also offered. They led us along the trail for another mile or so before diverting along yet another track. Eventually, we reached a clearing where some cars were parked. When my father strode into view, I cried out and ran toward him. Within seconds, I was wrapped in his arms, and the trauma of everything I'd experienced felt almost worthwhile. A genuine hug from my dad was so rare that I reveled in the sensation.

Mom appeared next, followed by my sister, Jasmine, and I thought my heart would break. "I didn't think I'd ever see you guys again," I sobbed, my eyes darting between each of them.

When a blanket was draped around my shoulders, I gripped it tightly, appreciating the warmth. Across the way, Holly's blanketed figure was surrounded by her family while a jumble of voices rang out around us.

"We were so worried about you," Dad said, his concerned eyes never leaving mine.

Tears flowed across my cheeks. Mom was crying too. My relief at being saved was so immense that I couldn't put it into words.

"These girls will be suffering exposure and dehydration," one of the rescue volunteers emphasized. "They should be taken to the hospital and checked."

Mom nodded her head. "We'll go there now. And we can't thank you enough. You've all been truly amazing."

"It's our pleasure," the man responded. "We're just happy the girls are safe."

Dad shook the hands of the various people standing by. I saw Holly's parents do the same. When a van belonging to a news crew pulled up, a reporter jumped out and hurried toward us, followed by a cameraman. Dad shuffled forward to speak to the reporter while Mom led me to our car. I waved to Holly before tumbling into the back seat, where I watched my father in action. He gestured animatedly as he spoke, and I wondered what he was saying.

By the time he climbed into the car, his worried

demeanor had turned to one of fury. "What happened up there? How did you girls get separated from the group? You were supposed to be properly supervised. I'm submitting a formal complaint to the school board. Your teachers were responsible for your safety, and losing two students is a disgrace. Which is exactly what I told the journalist!"

Mom's worried gaze slipped between my dad and me. "Shh, Caleb. Let's not get into that now. Ronnie's back safe and sound; let's focus on that."

"I'm not just letting it go," Dad ranted angrily as he started the car and reversed onto the gravel road. "Hopefully, the press gets behind me. The school has to be held accountable."

"Dad freaked out at Mrs. Jensen yesterday," Jasmine snickered. "Wish I'd seen her reaction."

Mom tried to turn the focus back to me. "We were so worried about you, Ronnie. We didn't sleep last night, and we were back here first thing this morning. Those search and rescue volunteers are truly incredible. They searched until dark last night then started again before sunrise. Do you know they even organized a helicopter?"

"Which will cost the taxpayers a fortune!" Dad continued to rant. "The school should have organized more people to supervise such a large group of kids. I'm telling you, it's unacceptable."

"An extra support teacher was supposed to come along, but she got sick at the last minute," I mumbled back.

"She should have been replaced!" Dad grunted. "And now we'll have a hospital bill to pay. Well, I'm going to send it to the school. They can cover the cost." He gave the steering wheel an aggressive yank, and the car skidded around a corner, throwing me against the door.

Mom leaned over and gently patted my knee. "Your father didn't get any sleep last night. He's very tired."

"*He's* tired?" I huffed back.

Mom ignored my remark and quickly added, "You

must've been terrified, Ronnie. Thank goodness Holly was with you."

"Where did you sleep?" Jasmine prodded. "Weren't you freezing up there?"

I let out a sigh, the memories tumbling back. "We found our way to the base of the mountain before dark, but we were lost, and we couldn't get service on our phones. So we huddled under a tree until morning. It was the scariest night of my life. This morning, we seemed to be walking in circles. We thought we'd never get out of there."

"Did you hear the helicopter?" Jasmine asked. "It was searching for ages."

"We caught glimpses of it through the trees this morning. When it skimmed past us and kept going, we thought we were doomed." Too exhausted to talk anymore, I turned my head to the window, and my eyes fluttered closed. Visions of spending the night, huddled up to Holly with only some low lying tree branches to shelter us, invaded my thoughts.

My father's angry rant broke through the silence and continued until we reached the hospital, where I was ushered into the emergency room. I spotted Holly already being checked by a doctor and offered her a wave. I was guided to a bed in a separate cubicle with my family gathered around me. My mom's worried frown furrowed her brow as she looked on.

Dad paced the floor, pausing to listen when the doctor explained that I was okay apart from a few cuts and scrapes on my arms and legs. I just needed to go home and rest. My dad's expression was a mixture of emotions. I knew he'd been terribly worried about me. But his focus right then was on our hospital insurance. It was an expense he couldn't afford, and he'd allowed it to lapse, which meant the cost of my visit would have to be paid for.

His gaze drifted to the bandage covering the large scrape on my left leg. When his eyes lifted to mine, I saw the sympathy there. It seemed he was finally focusing on the trauma I'd been through. Rather than every other detail that had been swirling through his head.

As I hobbled from the emergency room and out onto the street, I wondered if I could play on his sympathy. Junior Prom was the following week, and the summer break would follow. If my father could put aside his threats to keep me grounded for the months ahead, then my overnight wilderness adventure would be worth every ounce of trauma I'd suffered. In fact, if it meant I could go to Prom as well as have my freedom for the summer, I'd willingly go through the whole saga again.

CHAPTER EIGHT

Ali

I skimmed over the instructions Ms. Harris had added to the whiteboard. Everyone else had begun writing, but I found it difficult to focus. Ms. Harris had been called to the office, and a replacement teacher named Miss Teresi had taken her place. All the while, my insides churned with a mixture of relief and guilt. Relief that Ronnie and Holly were okay, and regret that I was responsible for their ordeal. Added to this was the genuine threat of Sammi spreading the news she'd heard. The girl was hopeless at keeping secrets, and my brain ticked over, searching for a solution.

My thoughts were still in chaos when Ms. Harris returned about thirty minutes later. I looked up from my work to see her eyes red and swollen, as though she'd been crying. I nudged Casey and nodded in our teacher's direction. Ms. Harris turned her back on the class and carried on a hushed conversation with the replacement teacher. With her head lowered, and her hair covering the side of her face, Ms. Harris picked up her laptop and purse and carried both items from the room.

"Where's Ms. Harris going?" Sammi called out. "And why is she crying?"

Everyone's eyes swiveled to the front as Miss Teresi tried to stammer an explanation. "Ms. Harris isn't feeling very well. I don't think she'll be back today. Now please get on with your work."

I glanced worriedly at my twin. "I wonder what's wrong with her. Do you think it has something to do with Ronnie and Holly?"

Casey shrugged, but I saw the worry in her features, and my anxiety spiked once more. Something was wrong, and my instincts told me the Ronnie – Holly drama was far from over.

When a curious murmur rippled through the room, Miss Teresi spoke again. "No more talking, guys. On with your work, please."

I put my head down and tried to concentrate, but when the session ended, I still hadn't finished the writing task and knew I'd have to complete it for homework. The title stared back at me…My most memorable Middle School Moments. Twenty-four hours earlier, I would have listed being voted school captain as number one. But overnight, that had changed. Number one was now the fact that I'd caused two of my classmates to become stranded in the wilderness, leading to a widespread land and air search to find them. I should have been looking forward to my final days of the semester, especially with the celebrations ahead. But instead, I was overwhelmed with worry and fear.

At the end of recess, Sammi pushed through the crowd and gripped my arm. I turned to her in alarm. "What are you doing?"

"I just heard something I thought you should know."

Normally, I wouldn't be interested in Sammi's gossip, but I sensed she had something important to say. "What is it?" I pressed.

She took a quick peek over her shoulder to ensure no one was in earshot, which wasn't common practice for Sammi Brownstone at all. "I was in the library, and I overheard Ms. Harris speaking with Mrs. Hansen," she explained.

I nodded my head, wishing she'd get to the point. I'd often seen Ms. Harris and our library teacher together. They were good friends. "Okay, go on."

Her eyebrows lifted high on her forehead as she spoke. "Ms. Harris is in trouble because Holly and Ronnie went missing yesterday."

My jaw fell open. I now knew why our teacher had been crying. "But it wasn't her fault they got lost."

"Exactly. And now Ms. Harris is worried she might lose her job."

My stomach plummeted to the ground. "What? Surely, that won't happen. It wasn't her fault!" I repeated.

Sammi shrugged. "The girls' parents are freaking out because Holly and Ronnie could have died up there. Mrs. Jensen is freaking out, too."

I gulped down the bile at the back of my throat as Sammi waited for a response. I was amazed that she hadn't spread the gossip around the school yet. It wasn't like her. "Have you told anyone else?" I pressed, needing to be sure.

"You're the first."

"Are you going to tell anyone?"

She shrugged her shoulders, and I knew I was in trouble. The news would eventually circulate, all of it, including my part. I had no choice but to admit the truth. Added to that, I couldn't stand by and let Ms. Harris take the blame. If she lost her job, I would never forgive myself.

"Is Ms. Harris still in the library?"

"I don't think so," Sammi replied. "I heard her say she's going home."

I swallowed the lump in my throat. "I need to speak to Mrs. Jensen."

Sammi's expression brightened. "Can I come with you?"

I didn't want Sammi hanging around and making things worse. "It's better if I speak to her on my own. But can you please not say anything to anyone. I need to get this sorted out."

A pleased smirk crossed Sammi's face. "Are you going to tell her what you did?"

I nodded again. "Promise you won't say anything."

"I promise."

I couldn't guarantee that Sammi would follow through. But there was nothing I could do about that now. Grabbing my sister's arm, I pulled her aside while Brie and Alexa shot curious glances our way.

"I need to talk to you," I murmured quietly and hustled Casey into a corner of the corridor away from the surge of students making their way to class. When I repeated Sammi's news, Casey heaved in dismay. "I need to own up," I told her. "I'm going to see Mrs. Jensen now."

"I'll come with you," Casey insisted. "I'm just as much to blame."

I gave my head an adamant shake. "I'm the one responsible, and I have to deal with it. Can you please tell Mr. Grover I'll be late for computer lab?"

Without waiting for her reply, I turned on my heel and scooted toward the office, my stomach churning faster with each step.

CHAPTER NINE

Casey

When Ali finally reached the computer lab, I could tell she'd been crying. I tried to push her for information, but she answered with a shake of her head. She then turned her eyes to the computer screen in front of her.

Jake sat on the other side of me. He and Mike were engrossed in their PowerPoint presentations and hadn't noticed that Ali was upset. Our task was to take bullet points from the writing we'd just done for Ms. Harris and add photos and graphics to illustrate our years at Middle School.

"It's a memento of your time here," Mr. Grover explained to us. "Something you can look back on in years to come."

It was a fun activity, and everyone was absorbed. We had access to the photos taken during various events over the past three years, and laughter filled the room when funny images were discovered. Everyone was enjoying the activity — everyone except Ali and me.

My head whirled with questions, but as we were locked into the lesson for a double period, I was forced to wait until the next break before I could speak to Ali. I didn't dare push for information with so many listening ears surrounding us. Sammi, in particular, was on alert. She knew enough already. We didn't need to add to the gossip she was already sure to spread.

Ali and I joined Brie and Alexa when the lunch bell rang; both the girls were concerned for my sister. We walked to the courtyard together and chose a private area where we could talk.

"What did Mrs. Jensen say?" I prodded Ali gently.

Ali's eyes welled as she spoke. "She's shocked and disappointed. And she couldn't believe I would do something so irresponsible. I tried to tell her the track was just a detour and that it linked up with the main one, but she wouldn't listen."

"Did you let her know the girls were constantly teasing you, and you wanted to get back at them? She recently suspended Ronnie because of what she did to you and Alexa. She knows how bad Ronnie can be."

Ali nodded. "Kind of. But she said she was tired of all the petty bullying. She pointed out that I was school captain and supposed to be a role model. Instead, I put my classmates' safety at risk. She went on and on about how dangerous it was for them to be left on the mountain on their own. Especially overnight. As if I didn't already know that." With a swipe of her wet cheeks, she exhaled loudly. Brie and Alexa sat silently beside me; no one knew what to say.

"She also went on about the search and rescue volunteers who'd spent their time scaling the mountain." Ali was on the verge of tears, and her voice wobbled. "Apparently, the helicopter search cost a ton of money. She didn't say how much, but I'm guessing it must have been ridiculously expensive. I was worried Dad would have to pay for it, but she said that wouldn't be the case."

The situation seemed to be snowballing with each word. "What about Ms. Harris?" I asked. "Will she be in trouble?"

"Mrs. J. said there'll be an investigation as our class was her responsibility. But Ms. Harris isn't to blame, and she won't lose her job."

"Lose her job?" Brie scoffed in alarm.

"That's what Sammi told Ali," I clarified. "Sammi was probably exaggerating. You know what Sammi's like."

"So, what happens now, Ali?" Alexa asked. "To you, I mean?"

Ali's eyes welled with more tears, and she brushed them away. "Mrs. Jensen is going to call Mom and tell her what I did. She said there'd be consequences, but she'll need time to think the matter through. What if she decides to expel me? If that happens, I won't be able to graduate. Imagine how that will look on my school record. Imagine if it ends up in the news! Mom and Dad will ground me forever over this. I'll never be allowed out of the house. Not even for Prom night!"

My breath caught as Ali's words registered in my head. Of course, the most important factor was that Holly and Ronnie were safe. But the roll-on effect for Ali could be horrendous. "I should have spoken to Mrs. Jensen too," I told her.

"Stop saying that, Casey. It was my idea. You even tried to call Holly back, but they'd already disappeared. I'm the one who's at fault." She buried her head in her hands and let out a muffled sob.

I turned to my friends, my despair at Ali's situation overwhelming me. We all had so much to look forward to. Our graduation ceremony was one of the highlights, and Ali and I, along with the two boy captains, had all been asked to make a final speech. We then had the dance. It was the hot topic that everyone was talking about it. Ali and I had already bought our dresses, and they hung in our closet at home.

Ali had been hoping Mike would ask her to be his partner. Although she refused to admit it, even after everything that had taken place, I was certain her crush on Jake's cousin was still alive.

I'd also recently noticed her flirting whenever she hung out with Sai. I'd questioned her, and she brushed aside my comment, saying it wasn't true. She suddenly seemed to be thriving on his attention, which was very confusing. I wondered if Ali really knew what she wanted or if she was as confused as me. Had she decided that because her fourteenth birthday was only a few months away, she was now ready for a boyfriend? I really couldn't be sure. Regardless, she couldn't miss out on our Junior Prom.

"Mrs. Jensen loves you, Ali," Alexa maintained. "You made a mistake, and you owned up to it. And besides, you have a perfect record. She's not going to expel you."

"I agree," Brie chimed in as she rubbed Ali's back in an effort to comfort her. "Ronnie and Holly are both okay. Hopefully, everything will sort itself out, and we can all enjoy our last two weeks of school."

As much as I sided with Brie and Alexa, there were other things to consider. Once our parents heard of Ali's involvement, she would be in a lot of trouble. And when Ronnie and Holly learned the truth, they'd be sure to retaliate.

I kept my thoughts to myself while hoping Brie was right and the situation did turn in Ali's favor. Remembering that things usually resolved themselves where my twin was concerned, I prayed this was another of those occasions.

CHAPTER TEN

When my phone started beeping with texts and Instagram DMs from the kids at school, I stared wide-eyed at the endless questions and comments.

Are you ok?

We heard u were rescued. We were so worried.

Where did u get 2? U just disappeared. Everyone was freaking out.

So happy ur safe.

Ur on the news. U guys r famous now.

How are you? Must've been so scary being out there all night! So good they found you!!

Although I was exhausted, I suddenly felt like a

celebrity and was unable to sleep. After scoffing down the large plate of scrambled eggs my mother had cooked, along with three slices of toast, I'd headed to the bathroom for a much-needed shower. I then climbed into bed, intending to go straight to sleep but was distracted by the messages on my phone. Everyone at school had heard the news, and I was grateful for their support. It also made me feel popular and special.

I checked with Ronnie. She'd also received a heap of messages and was just as thrilled. But when I read Sammi's text, I frowned at the screen. *Glad u guys are ok. Everyone was worried. Did you hear that Mrs. J. freaked out at Ms. Harris? She might get fired now. I saw her crying.*

What? I asked. I was aware that my parents and Ronnie's both blamed the school for the lack of supervision, but Ms. Harris shouldn't lose her job.

It's so unfair. It wasn't her fault you were sent along the wrong trail, Sammi replied.

I froze, my mind ticking over. *What do u mean?*

After several seconds, there was no response, so I asked again. *Sammi, what do u mean we were sent along the wrong trail?*

Bell just rang. Gotta go.

I reread her words and thought back to the moment we reached the fork. Ali had pointed to the right and told us to go ahead. What happened next was a blur, but I didn't remember ever hearing her footsteps behind ours.

Further along that track, we'd veered to the right again. I wanted to go left, but Ronnie insisted it was the wrong way. It could have been where we messed up. Even so, it still didn't explain Sammi's comment.

I forwarded her message to Ronnie, who texted back, asking if I thought Ali had sent us the wrong way. I couldn't think of any other part of the hike where Sammi's words made sense.

I replied to Ronnie with my suspicions, and she said she'd check in with Sammi herself. Sammi was the go-to

45

person when it came to news and gossip. If anyone were aware of the answers, it would be her. At the same time, though, she was renowned for spreading rumors that weren't true. Was she trying to cause trouble, or had she misinterpreted what had really taken place?

Finally overcome with exhaustion, I put the matter aside, deciding to deal with it later. Unable to keep my eyes open any longer, I switched my phone off and pulled the bedcovers up to my chin. Within seconds, I was sound asleep.

CHAPTER ELEVEN

Alexa

I asked Casey to keep me updated on the Ronnie – Holly saga once her parents learned of Ali's involvement. But it wasn't until later that evening when my phone buzzed with Casey's text.

It's bad! Mom and Chris both freaked out. They've grounded Ali. Not sure how long for. But I'm worried. I've never seen them this angry before.

I stared at the screen in dismay. It wasn't the result I'd been hoping for, and I sent back a row of upset emojis then dropped my phone onto the bed. While Ali's idea had been reckless, she'd acted on the spur of the moment, and I could

47

relate to that. I'd heard the bragging from Holly and Ronnie. It irritated me, so I knew it had to be bothering Ali. I understood her reaction completely.

I was also guilty of making spontaneous decisions where Ronnie was concerned. When I found Damon's phone in the school garden and noticed Ronnie's name in his list of Instagram followers, I'd jumped at the opportunity to prank her. While the twins had spurred me on, it had initially been my idea, and I'd happily kept the phone, pranking Ronnie for as long as possible.

Her bullying and mean behavior were so hurtful that it would easily motivate Ali to retaliate, just like I had done. Added to this, Ali hadn't deliberately caused Ronnie and Holly to lose their way. It was pure chance that they'd veered in the wrong direction, and hopefully, Mrs. Jensen would see things that way. I was also hoping the twins' parents would do the same thing. But according to Casey's message, that didn't seem likely.

Ali had been concerned about the news finding its way into the media, something else I could relate to. When my mother's theft was publicized, Aunt Beth had been frantic with worry over the consequences. Thankfully, it hadn't affected her job. Though, my aunt was still related to a thief, as were my brother and me. Something none of us was proud to admit.

Thoughts of my mom caused me to tense up even more. She'd contacted Tyler, asking him to spend the following weekend with her. It would be the first time he'd seen her since the court case. She even bribed him with the promise of a trip to Sea Life, the underwater world aquarium in town. Tyler had never been and was very eager to go there.

"Will Harry be going too?" I asked him, cringing at the thought of my mother's sleazy boyfriend anywhere near my brother.

"Mom said it'll just be her and me," Tyler replied. He'd obviously asked Mom that question already.

48

I was uneasy about him staying over. But the judge had given our mother custody of Tyler for one weekend per fortnight, and there was nothing I could do about it. Hopefully, it wouldn't become a regular event. Though Tyler was excited, and I shouldn't begrudge him for that. The woman was his mother, after all.

When my phone vibrated with another text, I remembered that I still hadn't replied to Casey's first message. Discovering the text wasn't from Casey with more distressing news, but a simple message from Damon instead, my mouth curved into a happy grin.

Watcha up to?

I tapped out a quick reply. *Trying to figure out what to wear to prom.*

I added a smiley face to the end and returned my attention to the computer screen on my desk where I'd been looking at dress styles and trying to make up my mind. Aunt Beth had offered to take me shopping on the weekend. She even suggested we go to the city where there were more stores to choose from. That way, there was less risk of turning up at the dance wearing a dress one of the other girls had purchased locally.

My aunt seemed even more enthusiastic than me and was determined to help me find something special. I was incredibly grateful. If I were still living with my mom, a new dress wouldn't be an option at all.

Damon's next message caused my heart to flutter. *You'll look pretty in whatever you wear.*

I hugged the phone to my chest and let out a quiet squeal. It was such a nice thing to say, and I couldn't believe the words had been directed at me. I was still struggling to accept the fact that we'd become close friends. It was so wonderful that it didn't seem real.

I reminisced over the moment he asked me to be his partner at the dance, and the butterflies in my stomach did another happy dance. He was so shy that he struggled to get the words out. When I nodded and said I'd love to be his partner, his beaming grin was like a ray of sunshine brightening an already sunny day.

"Oh my gosh, he's so cute," Casey shrieked when I told her afterward. "It'll only be a matter of time, and you'll be a real couple. Just wait and see."

My cheeks heated at her words. It was all so exciting. And the fun part was that Casey and Jake, and Elijah and Cora were also going to the dance in pairs. To be part of the couples' group was like a dream come true. Even though I wasn't ready to be official with Damon, crushing over a boy who actually liked me back made me all fluttery inside.

Over the past weeks, our entire group had grown close, and when Elijah offered us all a ride to the dance in his dad's twelve-seater minibus, everyone jumped at the chance. A couple of groups had already organized stretch limousines. That idea sounded very expensive and a little ridiculous for a bunch of thirteen-year-olds. It was only our Junior Prom, after all. In comparison, Elijah's minibus was an ideal alternative.

Finally returning my attention to Casey's message, I reread her words, and my excitement faded. Casey said she'd never seen her parents so angry. I chewed on my lip as I tried to think of a reply. We had graduation and Prom to look forward to. What if Ali wasn't allowed to take part? After that, we had the entire summer, and we'd already made a ton of plans.

I tapped my fingers thoughtfully on my knee, hoping the twins' parents would rant at Ali for a few days, then put the incident behind them. After all, we were in the final days of middle school, plus Ali was one of the school captains. She couldn't be banned from the events. Not over a silly prank that was never intended to do any harm.

I typed a message to both the twins, sharing my

thoughts. I then dropped my phone into my lap and stared thoughtfully at the wall opposite. Everything would work out. It just had to.

CHAPTER TWELVE

When Casey, Alexa, and I arrived at school the following day, we walked through the gates and found Ronnie and Holly surrounded by kids questioning them about their ordeal. I dreaded facing them. I also dreaded them learning the truth. I had no idea if Sammi had already blabbed or if she'd kept the details to herself. As soon as Ronnie spotted me in the crowd, however, I knew the answer.

She pushed through the group, her dark eyes blazing. "Is it true?"

"Is what true?" I mumbled back.

Her eyebrows lifted accusingly. "That you *deliberately* sent us along the wrong trail?"

Every pair of eyes had turned to me, and I gulped uneasily as Holly joined her friend, her face a mask of anger.

"It wasn't the *wrong* trail," I stammered. "It was just a detour, and it looped back onto the main track. I saw it on the map." They continued to stare accusingly, so I added lamely, "I didn't know it branched onto another trail as well. I'm really sorry. You weren't supposed to get lost."

"Because of you, we had to spend a night in the woods on our own," Holly raged. "It was the worst night of our lives. Do you have any idea what we went through?"

"Anything could have happened to us, Ali!" Ronnie was determined to state the obvious in case I hadn't considered it yet. "If we hadn't been found, we could still be walking those trails. No food, no water. We could have died out there!"

I tried to swallow the knot in my throat, but it was firmly lodged in place. "Like I said, I didn't mean for that to happen. You weren't supposed to get lost, and I'm really sorry that you did."

"We know you deliberately tricked us!" Ronnie spat, her eyes lowering to my school captain badge. She poked at it, shoving me back on the pavement in the process. "But it wasn't a *harmless prank!*" She emphasized the words, my words, the words Sammi had heard me say. Her voice grew louder and more forceful with each breath. "You're *supposed* to be a leader, a *role model.* You make out that you're *little miss perfect*, the girl who never does anything wrong. But this is the *true* Ali Jackson, and finally, *everyone* can see it!"

I lowered my head in shame as the two girls turned on their heels and walked away. The voices of Casey and Alexa telling me not to listen to Ronnie and that she'd eventually get over it fell on deaf ears. Ronnie was right. Responsible school leaders didn't make spontaneous decisions that had the potential to be life-threatening. As my dad had reminded me just that morning, every decision has a consequence. I'd already been grounded over the skate park incident with

53

Brodie and Jono. This latest drama added to my list of wrongdoings, and my parents were determined that I would face serious punishment this time.

"What you did could have had the worst consequence of all," Dad huffed before leaving for work, his disappointment filling me with even more shame.

So far, my involvement was missing from all the news reports, and I prayed it would remain that way. Along with the backlash from Ronnie and Holly, there were my classmates' stares and whispers to deal with. I didn't need the news spread amongst the local community as well. I'd already considered the ramifications ahead for me, and I knew I deserved them. I just wanted to rewind the clock and reverse my stupid mistake, so it didn't happen at all. If only that were possible.

As I walked to my locker, I felt several pairs of eyes following me. I passed Sammi, whose gaze locked on mine. She wasn't the slightest bit remorseful about sharing my secret after promising to keep it to herself.

"You're the one who did the wrong thing, Ali. Not me," she sniped.

I had no worthwhile response. Sammi was right. I was the one who'd made a mistake, and now it was time for me to pay.

CHAPTER THIRTEEN

Holly

I stood alongside Mike during band rehearsal. With my voice fully recovered from the viral throat infection that had plagued me for so long, I was finally able to reach the high notes again. The backing vocalists were grouped to the side, and I couldn't resist a smug grin.

The grad assembly would be our final performance, and after being reinstated as lead vocalist, the position I'd been promised in the beginning, I knew I deserved to be there.

After a few weeks of being in the wings while the others sang, I'd thought my chance to sing the lead was gone forever. But in the blink of an eye, everything had changed.

The grad assembly was a big deal. The entire school

population would be in attendance, plus all the parents of the graduating students; some important guests from the local community as well. It was our last opportunity to perform in front of everyone, and I couldn't wait.

When Mr. Flynn also suggested a duo performance from Mike and me, I felt like squealing with joy. Zoey complained that it wasn't fair, but Mr. Flynn held his ground. "You'll each get a chance to sing a solo section with the band, Zoey," he reminded her.

She rolled her eyes. "Yeah, for about five seconds."

I'd stifled my laughter at her response. And now, we were only days away from grad, and overnight, Ronnie and I had become celebrities.

"Since the hike, everyone wants to talk to us," Ronnie had snickered earlier. "Our Instagram accounts have totally blown up. I feel so popular, don't you?"

I nodded happily. And when I performed at the assembly, my celebrity status would spike even further.

Meanwhile, Ali's name continued to circulate on the gossip train, but not in a good way. I'd heard the whispered comments and noticed the looks from kids in the hallways as she passed. I hoped she was at least given a suspension, though Ronnie thought she should be expelled. What she did to us was unforgivable, and she deserved the worst of consequences.

After all the recent drama Ronnie had found herself in, she was pleased to see Ali in trouble for a change. "It's like a reward for having to put up with her for so long," she sniggered. "I wish it were both the twins. They're so painful."

Of the two girls, Ali was the one I wanted to see targeted, but regardless of what punishment she was given, she was already suffering. She barely opened her mouth during rehearsal, and she even kept her distance from Mike. She was probably riddled with guilt and totally embarrassed by all the negative attention, something she wasn't used to.

Even Casey seemed to be affected. Ali was her twin

sister, and Casey's name was constantly linked to the gossip. As Ronnie had said, to see them suffer was almost worth the trauma we'd experienced. Although truthfully, I never wanted to encounter such a terrifying ordeal again. Spending the night in the wilderness on the frozen ground, surrounded by animal noises and the fear of being attacked by some kind of predator, plus the fear of never being found, was a memory I'd prefer to forget.

I watched Mike end his guitar solo with a flick of his wrist and beamed up at him. He and Ali were no longer an item, so I didn't have to worry about competing with her. Busking through the summer with Mike would also mean spending lots of time with him for rehearsals and performances. My skin tingled at the thought.

As I helped him pack away the equipment, my thoughts drifted to Prom night, and I decided to broach the question that had been on my mind for the past couple of weeks. "Excited about Prom?"

He grinned back. "Yeah, it should be fun. My old school only has a graduation ceremony. So the dance is kind of new to me. But it'll be a cool way to end the year."

"Are you, uh, are you taking anyone?"

His lips quirked. "Nah, just going with the gang. We're all meeting at Elijah's. His dad's driving us in his minibus."

"That'll be cool. I heard some people are organizing stretch limos. That's a bit far-fetched, don't you think?"

"Yes!" he sniggered. "Stretch limos for middle schoolers? Crazy."

"Well, I guess I'll see you at Prom then. We'll have to have a dance together…last middle school celebration and all."

"Sure thing," he replied.

I nodded back, my insides buzzing. When I carried some equipment to the storeroom, I saw Ali watching me. I gave her a defiant glare and kept walking. She'd probably heard my conversation. If so, I was glad.

I'd been worried that Mike may have asked Ali as his date. Even though the pair were no longer official, I knew they were still close. But he hadn't asked her or anyone else. I packed the equipment away, my excitement bubbling over at what was ahead.

CHAPTER FOURTEEN

Casey

I sat in the courtyard with Jake beside me. Everyone was talking about Ronnie and Holly and also questioning me about Ali.

"Did she really send them along the wrong track? That's what everyone's saying, but we can't believe she'd do that," Cora quipped with a shake of her head.

The rumors had spread thick and fast. Fortunately, Ali was at band rehearsal and could avoid the stares of our classmates. Though she still had to deal with Holly, and that wouldn't be easy.

I tried to explain what had taken place and why Ali had made the choice she had, but no one seemed to understand. Cora and Lucy nodded their heads while Jake sat silently, refusing to comment. Even to my own ears, the explanation sounded lame. Although Ali had meant no harm, things hadn't ended that way.

Keen to change the subject, I switched topics to Prom night and what we planned to wear. My tension eased when Elijah described the bright blue suit he'd borrowed from his cousin. Everyone burst into laughter at his vivid depiction. He'd even organized a bowtie. In contrast, all the other boys were wearing pants or jeans and a button-up shirt with sneakers. I wondered what Cora thought of Elijah's outfit. He could be so quirky at times.

All the while, my connection with my twin was on full alert, and I sensed her despair. She'd been asked to see Mrs. Jensen as soon as band practice ended. We had no idea what would eventuate from that meeting, but things weren't looking good for Ali at all.

Jake slipped his hand into mine. "Don't worry," he murmured quietly. "It'll all blow over in another day or so. Everyone has grad and Prom to focus on. The hike drama will soon be forgotten." He could read my moods almost as well as my sister could, and I was grateful for his support.

He went on to ask for my opinion on the outfit he was considering for the dance, and I turned my attention to him. Try as I might, though, thoughts of Ali hovered in the background.

When the bell rang, I was distracted by the swarm of kids heading to the bus line. Croydon High school open day sessions had been scheduled for each day that week, and every eighth grader in the region who was planning to enroll was invited to attend. It was an opportunity to familiarize ourselves with the school layout and the classes on offer. Most kids in our grade were transferring there, while others had enrolled at Trinity Academy, the private school on the other side of town. They would attend the Trinity open day activities instead.

At some point, Ali, Alexa, and I would cross paths with

Brodie and Jono. We weren't looking forward to that. Seeing them on the bus each day was bad enough. But we were all eager to make new friends.

As I waited in line, I looked out for Ali but couldn't see her anywhere. I chewed on my lip, hoping Mrs. Jensen wouldn't force her to miss the afternoon. Although perhaps Ali would prefer it. That way, she could avoid the gossip and the pointed stares.

When I boarded the bus, I reserved the spot alongside me for Ali while Alexa and Brie grabbed a different seat. Ronnie and Holly boarded, and I watched discreetly as they strode confidently along the aisle. Aware of their growing celebrity status, I'd decided they were probably exaggerating every detail of their ordeal—anything for more attention. I knew I shouldn't think that way. I wouldn't want to experience what they'd been through, but I couldn't help my reaction.

Ali appeared soon after, and when she dropped into the seat next to mine, I noticed her red-rimmed eyes. "What happened?" I whispered. "What did Mrs. J. say?"

She sucked in a breath then heaved it back out again. "I have detention for every morning recess this week and next."

"No," I groaned. "What about the activity days?"

"I can go to the high school open days. She said I *need* to go to those. But I have to miss out on all the fun activities next week."

"What? All of them?"

A tear slipped from Ali's eye as she nodded her head.

"That's so unfair, Ali."

"Mrs. J. said that I'd *disappointed her to the utmost!*" Ali mimicked the principal's voice as she spoke. "She said I'd impacted the school's reputation and the reputation of the teachers who were present on the day. She's terribly upset that I've ended middle school on such a terrible note. She also said my behavior could affect my future if it were added to my school record. But as I've been a model student…until now...she'll skip that detail."

I could feel my sister's pain. It transferred to me and wound through my veins. I had been praying Mrs. J would let her off with a reprimand. Obviously, that wasn't the case; far from it. We sat quietly for the rest of the trip, each of us left to our thoughts while enthusiastic chatter carried on around us. Hopefully, Ali could enjoy our high school experience. If nothing else, it would be a distraction.

I was still conscious of her angst when we stepped off the bus, but we were soon divided into groups of ten and quickly became absorbed in our new surroundings. Brie, Alexa, and I managed to stay together. We were taken on a tour of the grounds by a senior student named Destiny, a girl whose head was covered in a mass of gorgeous black braids that hung to her waist. As we walked, she gave us a running commentary, and I listened with interest. I took particular notice of the badge labeled with the words *Student Body Vice President* that was pinned to her shirt.

It also caught Ali's eye. She'd already discussed the idea of joining the student council and had hopes of being voted class president when the time came. I hoped the recent drama wouldn't stop her from pursuing that idea.

When a bell signaled a change of period, the corridor was suddenly swamped with high schoolers and other eighth-graders.

"Ooh, he's cute," giggled a voice behind me. "I turned to see Zoey Alcott pointing to an older boy passing by.

"So many good-looking guys at this school," her friend, Kahli, remarked.

I did a quick scan of the group they were referring to and had to agree. A few of them were very cute. I prodded Ali and lifted my eyebrows. "Plenty of talent at this school, Ali."

She grinned back, the first smile I'd seen on her face in what seemed like days. I was pleased to see she'd managed to switch her focus, and my spirits began to lift.

Our freshman year would include many new faces,

kids from other schools we didn't know. There'd be the older students too. I'd already teased Ali about the new boys she would meet. But she'd laughed off my comment. For the time being, she claimed she was content to be friends with Mike and Sai. Even though I'd noticed there was still some kind of love triangle going on between them, something she refused to admit to me and also to herself.

Unfortunately, though, Mike's family planned to move back to their country property during the summer. Their new home would be completed, and Mike was expected to attend his local high school. Something he wasn't pleased about. He'd made many close friends amongst our group, friends he was reluctant to leave behind and who were also sad to see him go. Jake and Ali would miss him the most.

As Croydon High offered an extensive music program, it was an added incentive for Mike to stay. But that would involve a long bus ride, something his parents wanted him to avoid. Meanwhile, he was permitted to attend the Croydon High open day sessions. Though they would only highlight everything that he'd miss when he left town.

I couldn't imagine losing Jake to another school. High school was an adventure he and I were eager to share, and we were so lucky to have that opportunity. When he passed me in the corridor, he lifted his hand in a wave and smiled. I beamed back, my heart warming at the very sight of him.

As we walked, Zoey continued to prattle on behind us. Her focus was on the cute boys who happened to catch her eye. Her main aim for her freshman year was to find a boyfriend. It seemed to be her number one priority and all she could talk about.

When we were led into a large auditorium filled with tiered seating, I slipped into a seat next to Jake. Scanning the crowd, I spotted Ronnie and Holly seated toward the front and was glad to be separated from them and their scathing looks. While they had every right to be upset, I wanted to put the whole debacle behind us. Unfortunately, though, the two girls weren't yet ready to move on.

When the booming voice of Principal Morelli asked for everyone's attention, the noisy room was soon shrouded in silence. Shifting my focus to the stage, I zoned in on everything the principal had to say.

CHAPTER FIFTEEN

Alexa

Some of our group was sad to be finishing middle school, but I couldn't wait for what was in store and listened eagerly as Principal Morelli discussed the various programs on offer.

As Croydon High catered for academically gifted kids and kids who were sports oriented, I knew it was the ideal school for me. While Aunt Beth had pushed me to apply for a spot in the academic class, I wasn't sure my grades were good enough. They weren't the standard of Ali, Sai, and the other super-smart people in our class. Ali, in particular, was a stand-out A student and would most certainly be accepted. Whereas I didn't think I'd cope with the pressure that such a class would entail.

I'd previously learned that Physical Education was offered as an elective subject, rather than just a mandatory one-off class per week. As sports was an area I loved and excelled at, I would definitely choose PE as one of my primary electives.

Luckily, Uncle Vern shared my point of view. "There needs to be a balance," he reminded my aunt. "Alexa needs a good education, but some fun subjects will help her to enjoy high school."

Aunt Beth was only concerned with academics. She'd been a top student at school and had since earned a couple of university degrees. Luckily, Uncle Vern had my back. Otherwise, my aunt would push me to choose complex subjects like Physics and Chemistry. I wasn't even interested in science, so those topics didn't appeal to me at all.

Damon was aiming for a college football scholarship when he finished high school and was eager to participate in as much sport as possible. When Principal Morelli mentioned the sports program, I saw Damon sit up and take notice. It would be even more fun to share classes with him, and I hoped our schedules worked out that way.

Principal Morelli ended his spiel and introduced us to some of the headteachers, who explained the various clubs on offer. We learned that these included robotics, anime, rugby, and movie clubs, just to name a few, and an excited murmur rippled through the audience. Croydon High sounded even better than I'd anticipated, and I realized it deserved its reputation as one of the top high schools in the state.

We were introduced to the freshman guidance counselor next. She was a very pretty young woman with wavy dark hair that cascaded over her shoulders. She'd also made an impression on Jonah, who was sitting in front of me.

She's so hot were the words I heard him mutter in Elijah's ear. Elijah grinned in agreement and muttered something I didn't catch. I rolled my eyes, all the while wondering if Cora had overheard. She and Elijah had grown much closer, and I didn't think she'd appreciate Elijah obsessing over one of the teachers.

When the information session ended, we were directed outside to a large courtyard to eat lunch. Everyone scrambled for a seat in the various nooks and crannies. As I pulled my lunchbox from my bag, I noticed Damon nearby with his friends. His brown eyes crinkled at the sides when he smiled at me. I smiled back, aware of the butterflies stirring inside me.

"I often see him looking at you," Cora prodded with a grin.

"Oh stop, it," I giggled. "We're just friends."

"Sure, you are," she teased.

I blushed at her words and was pleased when she changed the topic to the prom dress that she'd bought the afternoon before. Lucy and Brie joined in the conversation and showed us some photos of the styles they'd chosen. Casey looked over my shoulder, and we commented on each one. I mentioned my aunt's idea to go shopping in the city on the weekend, and the girls suggested some stores I should try. They then went on to discuss hairstyles. We'd heard some girls in our grade had made salon appointments and were preparing for a complete make-over. None of us were bothering to go to such lengths. It was only a middle school dance, after all, not our Senior Prom. When that time came, maybe then we'd go all out.

When I noticed Ali sitting silently opposite, I studied her downcast eyes and the way she was scraping the toe of her shoe across the pavement. She pretended not to be listening, but I knew she was taking in every word. I tapped Casey's arm and nodded toward her twin. Casey looked in Ali's direction and sighed. Ali should have been a part of our conversation, but instead, she was avoiding it, and we both knew why. Casey tactfully changed the subject to the elective sessions scheduled for the afternoon, and the dance was momentarily forgotten.

When a teacher arrived and began calling names from a list, we found ourselves shuffled into groups according to the electives we'd previously nominated. Ali and Mike joined the Arts group, and I hoped Mike would help to cheer Ali up. Unfortunately, though, Holly scooted into place beside Mike and dominated his attention.

A sporty-looking senior directed the Physical Education group in the opposite direction, and I switched focus. Casey, Jake, Damon, Elijah, Jonah, and I walked to the gym, where we were asked to take a seat in the bleachers. Ronnie joined some girls from another school in a lower row. From where I sat, I could see the bandage covering her left leg. Several scrapes were also visible on her arm. Reminded of her ordeal on the mountain, I looked away, not wanting to think about what she and Holly had been through.

When I spotted a boy waving from across the bleachers, I waved back. Casey waved too, but it wasn't very enthusiastic.

"It's kind of awkward having Liam here," she mumbled in my ear. During triathlon training, Liam and Ethan had told us they planned to enroll at Croydon High, a fact Casey wasn't thrilled about. "After camp last summer, it's still a bit weird," she added quietly. "I get the feeling he might still like me. Imagine if he ends up in my PE class."

"But he knows you're with Jake," I reminded her. "And he and Jake get on really well."

Even though Casey agreed, she still found the scenario awkward. I'd noticed Liam watching her during the triathlon training sessions and hoped his interest wouldn't lead to problems down the track.

One person who did seem pleased to see the boys was Ronnie, whose eyes lit up the second she spotted them. I hadn't realized she knew them and wondered if Meg had introduced her. Everyone seemed connected somehow, which was very annoying if Ronnie was included in the mix.

When the PE teacher, a very fit-looking woman named Mrs. Wilson, began to speak, I turned my attention to her. After explaining what the freshman PE curriculum would include, she directed us onto the field outside, where she asked us to organize ourselves into teams of eight. Liam and Ethan hurried to join us, and the boys chatted while we waited for further instructions.

When Liam let loose with a sudden bombshell, my ears pricked. "So, Meg might be enrolling at this school."

"What?" Casey, whose mouth fell wide open, pushed into the conversation. "What did you just say?"

"Meg," Liam repeated. "We were chatting online the other night, and she said she might enroll here." Noticing Casey's frown, his eyebrows lifted. "Hasn't she told you?"

Casey shook her head. "She sent Ali a couple of brief texts after she left town, but we haven't really talked. What did she say? We thought she'd gone back to her old school."

Liam shrugged. "Her dad's been offered a permanent position here, so I think Meg and her mom will have to move back."

"But what about her grandmother? We thought she had to be cared for," Casey pressed.

"I think her grandma's fine now. So they don't have to look after her anymore," Liam replied. "I thought she would've told you all this?"

"We had a falling out," Casey mumbled. "We haven't really spoken to her since she left."

Casey turned worriedly to me. This was terrible news. If Meg ended up at our school, it would be the worst. "Don't mention this to Ali," Casey whispered in my ear. "She's got enough to worry about."

"Surely, Meg won't choose Croydon High?" I muttered back. "She made so many enemies when she was here. Maybe she'll enroll at Trinity Academy."

"Maybe," Casey replied, though I could tell she wasn't convinced.

Meg's family had rented a house in South Croydon, and I guessed her dad still lived there. Croydon High was the local school and the obvious choice for Meg. All the other high schools, including Trinity, were a long bus ride away. But they were still an option. Plus, Meg wouldn't be welcomed by our group. Ronnie certainly wouldn't welcome her either. It made sense that she'd choose another school. What I couldn't figure out was why she was messaging Liam. Although with Meg, nothing was ever straightforward.

I recalled the havoc she'd caused during her recent short stay. The idea of her returning didn't sit well with me at all. Just knowing she'd be living so close to us was bad enough. Having to face her at school each day would be intolerable.

CHAPTER SIXTEEN

Ronnie

When I noticed Liam and Ethan in the school gym, I couldn't help staring. I didn't know if they'd remember me, but I recognized them from Meg's birthday dinner the year before. Meg had also shown me their Instagram profiles and the stories they'd posted from the triathlon sessions. Both boys were cute, especially Liam, who I knew Casey had initially met at summer camp.

When I watched them chatting with Jake and his friends, my interest spiked. Damon, Jake, Elijah, Jonah, Liam, *and* Ethan...all doing PE. That would make the class much more fun. A pity Casey and Alexa were included. But when it came to sports, there was no avoiding those two girls. At least

Ali wasn't in the group. If she came near me again, I'd be tempted to spit on her.

Poor Holly had to put up with her presence amongst the Arts kids, though. A mixture of students interested in music, drama, and dance. It was just unfortunate Ali was involved. Hopefully, Holly could hang out with Mike, which would definitely irritate Ali. She deserved every thread of revenge we could throw at her.

Meanwhile, I had a new boy of my own to focus on, and when the teacher divided us into entirely new teams for relay races, I slipped into place behind Liam. I was pleased to learn that he did, in fact, remember me. He even remembered my name. During the first race, I heard him urging me on so our team would win, which spurred me to sprint even faster.

When I ran across the finish line first, he lifted his hand in a high-five. "You nailed that, Ronnie. Way to go."

I grinned happily back. Meeting new kids was refreshing. I'd already met a couple of friendly girls from other schools. A new boy who was friendly *and* good-looking added extra spice.

Liam and I compared notes on the electives we'd opted to try and realized we'd nominated a few that were the same. "We have a lot in common," I snickered. His encouraging grin caused my head to spin. Some new friends were exactly what I needed. So far, things were looking very good.

On the bus home that afternoon, Holly said she'd also met some fun people. What made her happiest was spending time with Mike.

"Ali didn't even try to talk to him," she explained with a grin. "I think she was trying to avoid me, so I had him all to myself. It was the best."

"Has Mike asked you about what happened to us?" I pressed, curious as to his perception of the hike disaster.

"He asked how I was, and he wanted to know how we coped on our own. But he didn't mention Ali, so I didn't either."

Holly and I were yet to learn the extent of Ali's punishment, and we hoped it would justify the seriousness of her actions. The twin who outwardly portrayed herself as the ultimate role model and the perfect student needed to pay for what she did, and the consequence should fit the crime. If not, my dad would be the first to complain.

However, when I arrived at school the following day, I found the gossip train on full steam once more. I discovered that Ali had been given lunchtime detentions until the end of the semester. She would also miss the fun activities organized for our grade in the final week. The news brought a smile to my lips. While I'd prefer to see her suspended or even expelled, I was satisfied with the consequence.

I had expected Mrs. Jensen to support Ali with excuses for her behavior and possibly even let the matter slide. Ali had always been our principal's favorite student. But I guessed my father's input had forced Mrs. Jensen to act. My dad was scary when he wanted to be. I knew that better than anyone.

Knowing that Ali had been dealt with properly allowed me to enjoy the rest of the week. Each session at the high school was as enjoyable as the last. I'd originally had low expectations, as Jasmine continually complained about how boring high school was. She'd also complained about the lack of hot guys in her grade. But it was already obvious I wouldn't suffer the same problem. There were plenty of classes to interest me. And several students worthy of attention. Liam stayed on my mind all week, and although I didn't see him very often, he was always very friendly.

When he added me on Instagram and suggested we hang out over the summer, I stared open-mouthed at my phone screen. While he hadn't asked me on an actual date, the simple fact that he wanted to hang out made my spirits soar.

Everyone always seemed to have boys interested in them. Even Holly. Was it finally my turn? Holly and I swapped notes, and it seemed that things were looking positive for both of us. Then, on Friday night, my father gave me the best news of all.

"Your mother and I have been talking," he said with a pointed look at me across the dinner table.

I stopped eating and sat up to listen. Ever since the field trip disaster, my dad's manner toward me had softened. I'd kept my fingers crossed, hoping it would lead to what I wanted most. But I hadn't dared to get my hopes too high for fear of disappointment.

He put down his fork, his expression solemn. "We thought we'd lost you for good this week, Ronnie, and it's made us rethink everything."

"Okay." My heart pounded as I waited for him to continue. Jasmine had also stopped eating; her attention focused curiously on our father.

"You have one week of middle school left." Dad lifted his forefinger to emphasize the point. "It all ends with graduation and then the Prom. We know it's a special time for kids your age, and you should have the opportunity to enjoy it."

"Does that mean…" I darted a look at Mom.

She nodded her head. "Yes, darling, you can go to the dance. We couldn't let you miss such a special occasion. And we also want you to enjoy your summer."

"What? So, she's ungrounded?" Jasmine snapped indignantly. "After all the trouble she was in at school with that Meg girl, you're letting her off?" She glowered at both our parents then turned on me. "That's not fair. You're supposed to be grounded for the whole summer!"

"She's already had her fair share of being grounded, Jasmine," Dad countered. "And I think she's learned her lesson by now. Haven't you, Ronnie?"

I nodded adamantly. "Yes, I totally have. I promise I'll never be in trouble at school again."

"Don't make promises you can't keep," Jasmine sniped before shoving a potato in her mouth.

My sister hated our father showing me any attention.

74

She was constantly sucking up, so he'd focus on her. Normally it worked, but this was my turn. I had no idea how long his good mood would last, and I wanted to take advantage. "Can I get a new dress for the dance?"

Mom didn't even hesitate. "Absolutely. We've already discussed it. We have a little money put aside. And I have the day off work tomorrow, so we can go shopping together."

'Yes!' I squealed, my excitement spilling over.

"I have some more good news to share," Dad rushed on, his smile now stretching across the width of his face. "I've been offered a position with a new start-up company in town. I'm still discussing details, but the salary is very attractive. So, go ahead and lash out on something extra special when you're shopping tomorrow."

"Oh my gosh!" I leaped from my seat and threw my arms around his neck. "Congratulations, Dad. That's amazing!"

It was the first time Mom had heard the news, and she jumped up to hug him too. The new job explained his good spirits. For me, the timing couldn't have been better. Jasmine gave him a half-hearted hug. I knew she was seething over the attention I'd been given, as well as his offer to spoil me with a new dress. But I didn't care. She'd already experienced Junior Prom. It was now my turn to enjoy mine, and Jasmine wasn't going to stop me.

Scooping a pile of salad onto my fork, I hurried through the remainder of my meal. I was eager to call Holly and share my news, my joy at what was ahead, bursting at the seams.

CHAPTER SEVENTEEN

Alexa

When I followed Aunt Beth into one of her favorite designer clothing stores on Saturday morning, I was immediately intimidated. The gloss and polish of the luxe décor added to the expensive clothing and put me completely on edge. It was a minimalist look, and rather than being overstocked like the chain stores were, the store was scantily filled with one-off designs that wouldn't be found elsewhere. The downward sweep of the saleswoman's eyes as she surveyed my aunt and then me certainly didn't help. These things didn't seem to register on Aunt Beth, who was in her element.

When I noticed the price tags, my mouth fell open. My

aunt often shopped at expensive stores, but the prices were ridiculous. Once again, though, Aunt Beth wasn't deterred.

"I have the ideal gown," the woman offered when Aunt Beth explained what we were looking for. "The color will look stunning against your niece's dark complexion."

Taking a long red gown from a rack against the wall, she held it in front of me. The layers of silky fabric fell in soft waves to the floor.

"I love the color," I told her. "But um, everyone's wearing short dresses."

"Short?" Aunt Beth countered. "It's your Prom night, Alexa. You need something special."

"I'd prefer a shorter style," I murmured back.

"What about this?" The saleswoman held up a satin dress in emerald-green with a high round neck and a layer of delicate lace covering the section above the waist.

I chewed on my lip and gave my head a slight shake. "It's a good length; it's just not really my style."

The woman lifted her eyebrows and nodded to the rack behind me. "Perhaps you'd like to browse the racks yourself. We have lots to choose from. Please take your time."

She then busied herself behind the counter, and without her hovering over us, I was able to relax a little. Aunt Beth scanned the selection, then pulled out a dress in a pretty shade of blue. I loved the color, but the tulle skirt wasn't what I had in mind.

"These dresses are all so expensive," I grimaced.

Aunt Beth smiled. "Don't worry about the prices, Alexa. It's not every day that I get to buy my niece a prom dress." She pulled out a few more options, but nothing appealed to me at all.

Aunt Beth was clearly unfazed. "Never mind. We'll try somewhere else."

I appreciated her patience and was relieved she wasn't pushing me to buy something I didn't like. We thanked the woman then headed back out to the street.

Aunt Beth pointed to a sign a couple of doors down. "Anastasia's Formal Wear is bound to have something you'll like, Alexa. And if not, we'll just keep looking."

Anastasia's was a replica of the store before it. Different dresses, but similar styles and nothing I'd feel comfortable in. My aunt had a particular type in mind. Disappointed that I wanted a short dress, she was suggesting flowing gowns in expensive fabrics that were just too formal for my liking. Once again, I shook my head at each style, and we soon found ourselves back on the street.

"Belladonna is a lovely store, and it's just up the road." Aunt Beth suggested. "Let's go there."

I nodded my head. She was trying to please me, and I didn't want to disappoint her, but the stores she'd chosen didn't offer what I wanted. Plus, I was reluctant for her to spend hundreds of dollars on a dress I may never have the opportunity to wear again. It was a total waste of money.

On our way, we passed a window display that caught my eye. I looked up at the sign…*Gossip Girl - Designer Wear and Special Occasion.* "My friends at school recommended this store," I told Aunt Beth, my excitement mounting.

A pale apricot-colored dress with a bodice sprinkled in a tasteful array of tiny jewels glittered in the sunlight. Next to it was another style in a gorgeous shade of pale pink. It was edged with sequins and flared out from the waist. The lengths of both dresses were mid-thigh, the exact length I was looking for. I turned eagerly to my aunt. "Can we go inside?"

"Yes, of course. It's your night, Alexa, and I want you to be comfortable. Let's see what else they have."

When we entered, I was surrounded by gorgeous styles with reasonable price tags. I asked the assistant if I could try my favorites from the window display. She searched for my size and hung the dresses in a cubicle at the back while I continued browsing.

"Can I please try this one too?" I asked her, pointing to a sleeveless dress with a round neckline and a glittery bodice.

It was available in both lavender and teal blue. "I'm not sure which color I prefer. Could I please try them both?"

"Absolutely," the sales assistant replied.

I spotted a couple more options and carried them to the cubicle. Aunt Beth was offered a seat, and one by one, I tried each dress on, asking my aunt's opinion on each style.

"They're all so lovely," I gushed. I swirled the skirt of the lavender dress and admired my reflection in the mirror, wondering if Damon would like it too. "I don't know which one I like most."

"I love that one." Aunt Beth gave a firm nod of her head. "The color and style are spectacular on you. I really love the teal blue as well."

So pleased she was happy with my choices, I studied my reflection for a moment longer. Deciding to take the lavender, I turned back to the dressing room. It was then that I found myself confronted with the person I least wanted to see. In her hand was the same lavender dress I was wearing.

"Ronnie…" I stammered.

Her eyebrows shot up in surprise. "What a coincidence. I didn't think I'd bump into anyone from school today, especially not in the city. And it seems we have the same taste." She nodded to the dress in her hand.

My expression soured, the dress losing all appeal. I no longer wanted it.

A woman who I guessed was Ronnie's mother hovered beside her. She gave Ronnie a questioning look. "A friend from school, Ronnie?"

Ronnie paused before answering. She and I definitely weren't friends. "Alexa is in my grade."

"How exciting for you girls!" Ronnie's mom exclaimed. "Junior High Prom night is so special. I still remember mine." She scanned the dress I was wearing. "That's the same dress Ronnie picked out. What are the chances."

"That's okay. I've chosen something else. If Ronnie wants this one, it's fine."

My head was reeling. Of all people to bump into, it had to be Ronnie Miller. My happy mood was shattered into tiny pieces.

Behind me, Aunt Beth got to her feet. "Hello, I'm Beth Johnson. Alexa's aunt."

"Hello," Mrs. Miller replied. "I'm Louise Miller, Ronnie's mom."

An arrogant smirk planted itself on Ronnie's face. "Alexa lives next door to Ali Jackson," she announced to her mother.

My stomach dropped. I knew what was coming next.

"Oh, my goodness," Mrs. Miller placed a comforting hand on Ronnie's shoulder. "Poor Ronnie and Holly. What they went through because of that girl's stupidity. Such disgraceful behavior, don't you think? And from a school leader! I hope she's punished properly. It was such a terrible ordeal for all of us."

Aunt Beth knew what had taken place during the field trip. I'd explained everything to her. She was also aware of Ronnie's ongoing bullying and how she and Meg had tried to frame me for stealing Ali's belongings. On the contrary, Ronnie's mother didn't appear to realize who I was. Even though Ronnie had been suspended over the incident.

"It must have been very traumatic for you, Ronnie," Aunt Beth said in answer to Mrs. Miller's remarks. "I'm glad you're okay. I also hope the bullying at school has stopped."

"Oh, there are some terrible bullies at that school," Mrs. Miller quipped, totally misunderstanding my aunt's meaning. "Let's hope our girls can make some lovely new friends at high school next year."

Ronnie knew my aunt was referring to her, and her smirk faded. "I think I'll try some dresses on," she said, suddenly eager to escape. She handed the lavender one back to her mother. "Can you return this to the rack? I've changed my mind. I don't like it at all."

She then moved into an empty cubicle and closed the

door. I glanced at my aunt. "I'll just get changed."

I quickly returned to my own clothes, gathered the dresses together, and followed Aunt Beth into the store.

"Did you make a decision?" Aunt Beth asked quietly.

I nodded my head and indicated the teal blue dress in my hand. I figured that because Ronnie had decided against the lavender, she wouldn't consider that style. Even though it was available in other colors. At least, I hoped that would be the case. To turn up at the dance in the same dress as Ronnie would be a humiliation I didn't want to contemplate.

Aunt Beth smiled. "Lovely choice, Alexa. The teal is gorgeous on you. You'll look beautiful on the night."

She took the dress from me and carried it to the counter. I carefully laid the other dresses aside and waited for my aunt to pay for the purchase. The assistant placed the dress carefully into a gold-threaded tote bag, tied the handles together with a strip of glittery ribbon, and passed the bag to me. "I hope you have a wonderful night at your Prom. I'm sure it will be very special."

"Thank you so much," I replied and followed my aunt from the store.

"So, that's Ronnie," she murmured as we headed along the street.

"Yep, that's Ronnie."

"Hmmm." She raised her eyebrows though she didn't say anything more.

We made our way to a shoe store that we'd passed earlier. As I tried some different styles, I worried Ronnie would show up and ruin more of my day. Thankfully, though, I managed to choose a pair of low-heeled strappy white sandals without Ronnie turning up at the door. We then made our way to a nearby restaurant for lunch. All the while, I remained on the lookout, just in case. But we didn't bump into Ronnie and her mother again.

By the time we'd arrived home later that afternoon, I'd put Ronnie's unexpected appearance to the back of my mind.

I'd previously promised myself not to feel intimidated by that girl, and it was a promise I needed to keep. With that mindset foremost in my head, I thanked my aunt for the day of shopping, telling her how much I appreciated the clothing she'd bought for me.

I climbed the stairs to my room and took my dress from the tote bag. Holding it up in front of me, I checked my reflection in the mirror. It was the most beautiful dress I'd ever owned, and I was thrilled with my choice. Kicking off my shoes, I replaced them with my new sandals. I held the dress up again and swayed from side to side as I studied my reflection once more.

The twins and I had already discussed the idea of getting ready for the dance together. Ali was fabulous at styling hair, and Casey and I had planned to rely on her for help. I'd already envisioned some bouncy curls. That would require straightening my unruly frizz, followed by the use of a curling wand. Ali owned one of those and was an expert at using it.

So far, the twins' parents hadn't mentioned Prom night, and we were desperately hoping they'd allow Ali to go. Even though she was officially grounded, the dance was a one-off occasion that she would never get the opportunity to experience again. We all had our fingers crossed that her parents would understand.

I snapped a quick photo of my dress, then sent it to Casey, eager to hear her thoughts. Thrilled at her impressed reaction, I put my outfit in the closet, then headed down the stairs to help Uncle Vern prepare dinner. As I walked, I sent Tyler a quick text, asking him about his day at the aquarium. Thoughts of my brother had been at the back of my mind all day, and I was hoping he was okay.

The fact that Harry was in the driver's seat when Mom arrived to collect Tyler that morning had made me ill at ease. I'd remained in my room, not at all interested in greeting my mother. Instead, I watched from the window as she walked with Tyler down the drive, her arm slung around his shoulders. She'd promised a weekend together, just the two of them, and I knew Tyler would be annoyed to see Harry there. He didn't like our mother's boyfriend. And neither did I. When I later mentioned the issue to Aunt Beth, I discovered that she was also concerned.

I hoped Tyler had managed to enjoy himself regardless. As long as he was safe was what mattered most. It wasn't until later that evening, though, that my brother finally responded to my message.

CHAPTER EIGHTEEN

I was so excited for my day at Sea Life with Mom that I woke up extra early. I wanted to be ready when she arrived, but when I walked down the drive and spotted Harry in the car, I froze.

"What's Harry doing here?" I asked quietly so only Mom could hear me.

She gripped tighter to my shoulders and urged me forward. "I thought it would be fun for us all to be together."

"But you promised it would just be you and me this weekend."

"I don't remember saying that."

She'd definitely promised, and I didn't understand how she could forget. She opened the car door and told me to climb in the back. I didn't want Harry there. I was supposed to be spending time with Mom.

As I waved to Aunt Beth and Uncle Vern, Harry pressed on the accelerator, and the car sped away. When Harry asked what I'd been up to, I told him about all the fun things I'd been doing with Uncle Vern. Mom said she didn't want to hear about that, so I talked about school instead. After a while, Harry turned up the volume on the radio, so I stopped talking and spent the rest of the trip playing on my phone.

The aquarium was super cool. I was able to forget about Harry and focus on all the awesome sea creatures instead. My favorite was the ocean tunnel. We were surrounded from above and on both sides by an oceanarium filled with sharks, rays, reef fish, and a heap of other interesting creatures. When a diver hand-fed the sharks, it was the coolest thing I'd ever seen.

On the way home, I asked Mom if we could go to Sea Life again sometime. But according to her, it was way too expensive. I didn't know she'd won tickets for us to enter that day. Without those, she said we couldn't have gone.

When we arrived at her apartment building, Harry climbed the stairs with us. "Are you staying for dinner?" I asked, hoping the answer would be no.

He scoffed as though I'd said something stupid. "Of course I'm staying for dinner. I live here now." Wrapping an arm around Mom, he pulled her to him and planted a sloppy kiss on her cheek, which made me cringe. "Haven't you told him yet, Charlene?"

My eyes flicked to Mom, and she grinned back. "I was waiting to surprise you, Tyler. Harry will be here all the time now, isn't that great?"

Harry kissed her again. This time on the lips. I felt like he was doing it on purpose just to annoy me. A sickly feeling crept into my stomach, and when Mom opened the front door, I dropped my bag on the floor and slumped onto the couch.

"Don't leave your bag there!" Harry grunted. "Put it in your room."

I felt like telling him not to boss me around. He wasn't my dad. But Mom nodded at me, urging me to do as he asked. So I did. My room still looked the same. The two beds were still in place, and I wished Alexa had come with me. I didn't want to be there on my own.

When I returned to the living room, Harry had started a PlayStation game, and I sat down next to him to watch. It was a new game, one I hadn't seen before. I picked up the cover and read the title. Bloodborne. The scenes looked scary, and I skimmed over the description.

Strong horror themes. Strong violence.

Hunt your nightmares, face your fears, and fight for your life with blades and guns. Discover secrets that will make your blood turn cold.

"This looks freaky," I told Harry.

"Ah, mate, it's the best," Harry replied as he sliced a zombie-looking character with a metal sword, and blood spurted all over the screen.

Aunt Beth would never allow that game in her house. It was rated M+, and I was only allowed G or PG.

"Can I have a turn?" I asked Harry. Mom had bought the PlayStation for me, and I should be allowed to use it. Even though the scenes were freaky, the temptation to play the game was too much.

Harry ignored me and sliced another character in half. My insides turned to mush. I always reacted that way when I saw blood. "I hope this doesn't give me nightmares," I told him.

"Kid, you need to toughen up."

I sat back on the couch and watched, the scenes becoming more and more bloodthirsty. Mom sat next to me, flicking through a magazine. After a while, I grew hungry and bored.

"What's for dinner?" I asked her.

She looked at me and smiled. "Pizza. I've been saving the vouchers till you arrived."

"Mega Meatlovers!" I yelped.

"That's not available with a voucher. Only the value pizzas are. But you love pepperoni. You can get one of those."

"Mega Meatlovers is much better. That's what Uncle Vern and I always order. We get the gourmet kind. It's the best!"

"Oi!" Harry snapped and scuffed the top of my head with his hand. "Don't bring that fancy pants attitude here. Be grateful you're getting fed."

Flinching, I scowled back. "I was just asking. You didn't need to hit me!"

"Tyler!" Mom warned.

I folded my arms angrily against my chest. My stomach rumbled as I imagined Alexa, Uncle Vern, and Aunt Beth sitting around the dining table eating one of my uncle's delicious meals. I suddenly wanted to be with them and wondered if I could ask Mom to take me back there. But something in Mom's expression told me that was a bad idea, so I didn't dare.

When I pulled out my phone and saw Alexa's message, a tear dripped from my eye. I brushed it away and typed a message back, pretending I was having a good time. I didn't want my sister to worry. And I didn't want my aunt and uncle to worry either. With my stomach grumbling, I stood up and went to my room, hoping Mom would order the pizzas soon.

I laid down on my bed and thought about Alexa's warning. She'd said the words a while back, but I still remembered them. *The money will eventually run out, and everything will change.*

Before the court case, Mom had plenty of money. At least that was how it looked. Since then, everything seemed to have returned to the way it used to be. Except my mom now

87

lived in an apartment with Harry, instead of a trailer with Alexa and me.

When I later heard Mom call me for dinner, I was ravenous. So was Harry, and he scoffed down a whole pizza on his own. I shared the other one with Mom. They weren't very big, and there was no dessert. I thought of the chocolate ice cream in the fridge at my uncle's house and how much I'd love a scoop. I reminded myself that I was only staying for one night, and the chocolate ice cream would still be there the next day…unless Alexa ate it all.

Before bed, I sent her a text asking her to leave me some, then I climbed under the covers and tried to fall asleep. But images of blood-sucking zombies oozing blood and gore from their eyeballs invaded my head, and my eyes popped open again.

CHAPTER NINETEEN

Ali

    I should have been looking forward to my final week of middle school. Activities were planned for most days. A trip to the cinema, an afternoon of competitive games on the football field, and even a full day at the local aqua park, complete with water slides and inflatable obstacle courses. But instead of taking part in all the fun, I was stuck in the school library, helping the librarian, Mrs. Hansen, catalog new stock and cover and repair books in preparation for the following year.

    My humiliation was rife as I went about each day, my head hung low to avoid the whispers and stares of classmates. Casey claimed the incident was behind us, but that wasn't true. It would follow me until school ended. I wished the summer break would hurry so I could finally escape.

Although Holly ignored me, I was aware of Ronnie's glares. I wondered if the girls were satisfied with my punishment. Ronnie was in a heap of trouble such a short time before, and our worlds had flipped in reverse. I'd taken her place as the offending student.

After a dull Monday afternoon in the library, while everyone else was occupied and having fun, I decided there was no point in even being at school. I should stay at home for the remainder of the week. Return for the grad assembly and the dance, then put middle school behind me.

When I broached the idea with my mom, opting to test her and hope for the best, she turned to me and frowned. "Ali, you're grounded. That means no dance on Friday night."

I had been hoping and praying she'd allow me to go. Casey and the others had all convinced me that my parents would relent. I wasn't going to give up easily. When my father entered the kitchen, I turned to him for support. "Dad, can I please go to the Prom? I have to be there. I'm one of the school captains, remember? And I already have my dress."

I pictured the sky blue dress hanging in my closet. The bodice was decorated in a pretty pink pattern, and a flowing pleated skirt was attached at the waist. My dusty pink sandals were the ideal accessory. I'd also bought blue ribbons for my hair and had experimented with a hairstyle, deciding on long curls draping down my back. To miss out on the opportunity to put it all together and join my friends would be devastating.

Dad sighed heavily, his eyes drifting to Mom then back to me before shaking his head. "I'm sorry, Ali. But you've brought this on yourself. You need to be punished."

"But I *am* being punished," I argued. "I have lunchtime detentions every day. I'm missing out on all the fun activities at school this week, *and* I was grounded all weekend. Casey slept over at Brie's house. Lucas stayed at Matt's, and I was

90

here on my own. For the *whole* weekend. Isn't that enough punishment?"

I could see my father softening, but Mom held firm. "You need to learn a lesson."

"Mom, I made a mistake. I know what Ronnie and Holly went through was terrible. I've apologized to them, and I totally regret what I did. It was a stupid decision, and I'll never make a mistake like that again. But I have to go to Prom. I just have to!"

"There'll be another prom. You'll have to wait until then."

"Senior Prom? But that's years away! I'll never get another chance to celebrate the end of middle school. I *have* to go!" Mom shook her head, unrelenting. "It's not fair," I sobbed. "The entire grade is going. I'm one of the school captains. I should be there."

Dad chewed on his lip. If it were up to him, I was sure I could sway him. But Mom was adamant. She turned her back and opened a recipe book, her focus switching to the pages in front of her.

"Dad?" I pleaded.

"Sorry, Ali." He lowered his head and joined Mom at the kitchen counter, signaling that the conversation was over.

"It's not fair!" I screeched and stomped my foot on the floor. "I hate you both!"

Lucas appeared in the doorway, his eyes wide. "What's going on?"

"Get away from me!" I shouted and shoved him aside so I could pass.

I ran along the hallway and up the stairs to my room, where I threw myself onto my bed. Casey was next door with Alexa, having fun, no doubt. Meanwhile, my life sucked, and Ronnie Miller and Holly Neumann were to blame. If only they hadn't pushed and pushed, I wouldn't have made the decision I had. Holly and Ronnie. I despised them equally.

My bloodshot eyes drifted to my bedside table, where a

photo of my adopted mom sat in a silver frame. A sob bubbled in my throat. If only she were here with me now. She would understand my point of view. But instead, I was stuck with a mother who refused to listen. I thumped my pillow with both hands, buried my head, and cried.

CHAPTER TWENTY

Holly

After a super fun final week at school, I woke on Friday morning with the anticipation of graduation and my performance at the ceremony filling my thoughts. Bombarded with a sudden rush of nerves, I decided to message Mike. When he reassured me that I would nail our songs and had nothing to worry about, I felt his positive energy pulsing through the phone. He believed in my ability, and I needed to do the same thing.

As I repeated his words in my head, I imagined myself on stage, my voice sounding better than it ever had before. The image caused a ripple of excited goosebumps across my arms, and I knew I'd be okay. Like a mantra circling my brain, I repeated Mike's words as I dressed in my chosen outfit and combed my hair, leaving it to hang loose over my shoulders. I popped my graduation gown over my head and grinned at my reflection in the mirror as I adjusted my cap. The day had finally arrived, and I was ready for it.

When I arrived at school, I hopped out of my parents' car and was confronted with a sea of royal blue graduation gowns. Ronnie stood amongst the crowd near the gate entrance, and I gave my family a quick wave before hurrying to join my friend. Her hair hung in shiny strands beneath her grad cap, and her blue gown contrasted strikingly against her dark features. After being ungrounded, she was ready to embrace her newfound freedom and greeted me with an excited hug. Pressing her face next to mine, she lifted her phone in the air and snapped a selfie. With my smile stretched broadly across my face, I pulled out my own phone and did the same thing.

The twins stood side by side in the group behind us. Dressed in their caps and gowns, the only visible difference between them was their hairstyles. Ali's signature braid hung over her shoulder while Casey's curls bounced around her face. When I looked more closely, I noticed something else. Casey was laughing and chatting with her friends while Ali stood quietly by, her usual confidence nonexistent.

We'd heard a rumor that she was banned from the Prom. If it were true, it would weigh heavily on her mind. But she deserved to be punished. And apart from being expelled or suspended, missing Prom was the best consequence of all. Being stuck at home while everyone else enjoyed the dance was a feeling I knew well. I'd experienced it myself during the fundraiser disco. Although, to miss Junior Prom was another level entirely.

I pondered the fact that Ali had once been my biggest rival. Now my world was surging ahead, whereas hers was shrouded in gloom and doom because of her reckless prank.

She'd brought it upon herself, and I had no sympathy.

When we were asked to form a line for the walk of honor, everyone shuffled into place, with the school leaders taking their spots at the front. The line snaked across the front lawn, and Mrs. Jensen beckoned us forward. It was a tradition for the graduating students to circle the grounds, passing by the teachers and younger students who lined the pavements ready with congratulatory high fives. We'd formed part of that crowd in the previous years, but now we were the stars.

We threaded our way around the school, and an exhilarated rush filled my veins. We'd reached the end of a special era, and there were exciting times ahead. Ronnie and I both had our sights set on turning fourteen and making a bunch of cool new friends. With Ronnie's new obsession over Liam Armstrong, she was very enthusiastic about starting high school.

When we entered the auditorium, however, my nerves resurfaced. It would soon be time for the band's performance, and as we waited for the ceremony to begin, the electric buzz filling the space mixed with my anxiety.

Mrs. Jensen stepped onto the podium and asked everyone to stand for the national anthem. A quiet hush filled the audience as we waited for the music to begin. My heart hammered in my chest as the music spilled out and everyone joined in the song.

Our equipment had been placed on the stage in readiness, and when the national anthem ended, the band members shifted into place. I stood front and center behind the lead microphone and looked out at the sea of blue in the front rows. To the side were the special guests, and behind them were the eighth-grade parents. Students from the lower grades sat at the rear. It was my biggest audience ever but performing was in my veins. It was what I wanted to do with my life, and regardless of my nerves, I was ready to sing my heart out.

Mrs. Jensen presented her welcome speech then

introduced the band. Pushing all nerves aside, I waited for Mike's opening chords and my cue to begin. I sang the first line, and when the other instruments and the backing singers kicked in, I knew we sounded more impressive than ever before. As promised, each of the singers had a chance to sing alone, but I had the lead role, the spot I'd dreamed of. All eyes were on me. I could feel them watching, and I drew confidence from deep inside me. We ended with the sound of whistles, cheers, and deafening applause from the audience. I met Mike's thrilled gaze with one of my own, my pride at being part of such an impressive group, reaching a crescendo in my heart.

When we filed off the stage, I slipped into the seat Ronnie had saved for me.

"You were amazing!" she whispered in my ear. "So proud of you."

Eternally grateful for her support, I acknowledged her with a beaming smile. I then sat back to listen to the speeches by Mrs. Jensen, various teachers, and some important community members. When the school captains were called forward to present their speeches, we watched Ali, Casey, Everett, and Mark climb the stage steps. Ali spoke first. As usual, she was flawless. Ronnie poked my side, and I caught the roll of her eyes as Ali went on about her years at middle school and her role as captain. She made no mention of being a leader or a role model. Ronnie and I both knew why. A tiny part of me felt sorry for Ali. Then I remembered the fear Ronnie and I had experienced on the mountain. With the memory still so fresh in my mind, my sympathy faded.

Casey followed with her speech. She was much more animated than her sister and even made some funny comments that caused everyone to laugh. Ronnie, on the other hand, remained straight-faced. Her animosity for both the twins remaining fixed in place. As Ronnie's best friend, I'd always supported her, but the twins were no longer a threat to me. I still had another song to perform, and it was my chance to shine.

With that thought in mind, I listened to the remaining speeches then followed my classmates onto the stage to accept my graduation certificate. When Mike and I returned for our duo performance at the end of the ceremony, I stepped up behind the microphone once more. The song we'd chosen was an audience favorite. With an upbeat tempo and inspiring lyrics, it was ideal for the occasion. I closed my eyes and let loose, my voice bursting forth like it never had before. When we finished to a standing ovation with almost the entire audience on their feet and cheering wildly, I'd never felt so proud.

Leaning into the microphone, Mike and I both shouted, "Time to celebrate!" We then tossed our graduation caps into the air.

Our classmates followed our cue and hurled their caps above their heads as well. Bubbling with joy, we all joined our families for the graduation feast that had been laid out in readiness outside the hall.

The excitement had only just begun. We still had the dance to look forward to, and my instincts were telling me it would be a night to remember.

CHAPTER TWENTY-ONE

Casey

    Later that afternoon, I followed Alexa to her bedroom, my arms laden with my prom dress and a bag containing everything I needed to complete my outfit. When I thought of Ali at home on her own, I was hit with a fresh surge of guilt. While I wasn't directly responsible for the field trip drama, the situation would have been prevented if I'd chased after Ronnie and Holly. I deeply regretted not following my instincts. Ali kept insisting I wasn't to blame, but the thoughts continue to swirl at the back of my head regardless.

    Gathering together everything I needed for Prom while my sister looked on had been awkward. I hated leaving her behind but getting ready in front of her was an uncomfortable thought for all of us. When Alexa invited me to her house instead, I accepted eagerly.

Although Ali was still happy to help with our hair, the idea seemed cruel, especially with Alexa and I prancing around in our prom outfits in front of her. Plus, we wanted to enjoy the experience, and to have any hope of that, we needed to distance ourselves from my twin.

I soon discovered Alexa's aunt was a fabulous hairstylist. She managed to smooth my springy curls into sleek waves that flowed over my shoulders, the effect exactly what I'd hoped for. She also transformed Alexa's naturally tight curls into bouncy long strands. With the addition of some pretty hairpins to clip up the sides, Alexa and I had individual styles that we were both thrilled with.

We then set to work with a little makeup and had fun helping each other apply some of Alexa's aunt's mascara to our eyelashes. A touch of lip gloss completed the look.

Alexa's teal blue dress was absolutely stunning against her complexion, and she really did look incredible. "You look amazing," I told her.

"Thanks, Casey. So do you," she replied, her smile radiant and making her look prettier than ever.

Checking my reflection in the mirror, I smoothed the folds of my skirt and adjusted my sleeves. I was particularly pleased with the style as well as the mint shade of the fabric and hoped Jake would also be impressed.

Finally satisfied, Alexa and I headed down the stairs and found her family in the midst of a card game in the front living room.

"Wow!" Tyler exclaimed when he saw us in the doorway. "You two look really pretty!"

Alexa and I exchanged pleased glances, beaming at her brother's reaction. Alexa had said he'd been acting out since returning from a weekend with his mother. That afternoon, though, he seemed settled and happy.

"Why, thank you, Tyler," Alexa replied.

Mrs. Johnson nodded with approval. "You really do look gorgeous."

"Stunning!" Mr. Johnson agreed.

I sent my parents a quick text, and a few minutes later, we were all grouped outside on the front lawn with my mom and Chris raving about how beautiful Alexa and I looked. A photo session followed with everyone snapping photos while Alexa and I posed for the cameras.

With the connection between my twin and me still in full force, my eyes were suddenly drawn to the upper story of our house, where I saw Ali at our bedroom window, watching us. She lifted her hand in a wave, her forlorn smile causing my stomach to clench. I waved back while sending a silent message across the airwaves. *The dance won't be the same without you.* I had made the same remark numerous times already, and I wanted to remind her that I was still thinking of her.

Conscious of her watching, I posed for a couple more photos then slipped into the back of Mr. Johnson's car, taking care to smooth my dress beneath me. When we reversed down the drive, I felt as though a piece of me were missing, and my heart went out to my sister once more.

Alexa gave me a reassuring smile. Although she sympathized with Ali, we had an exciting night ahead, and she wanted me to enjoy it.

We were amongst the last of our group to arrive at Elijah's house, and as soon as Jake saw me, his eyes lit up. "Whoa, Casey! You look so beautiful!"

Thrilled at his words, I beamed back. "Thank you, Jake. And you look very handsome!"

Dressed in a white button-up, long-sleeved shirt with new navy pants and tan shoes, he was even better looking than usual. I was so proud to be his girlfriend.

Brie was the only other person in our group with an official boyfriend, but Wyatt had his own school dance to go to. Though Brie didn't mind and was ready to enjoy the night with her friends.

Except for Elijah, all the boys were dressed similarly to Jake, with Sai adding a vest and a tie. The style suited him, and I wished Ali were there to see how handsome he looked.

Elijah wore his cousin's bright blue suit and matching bowtie and opened the car door with a swish of his arms. "After you," he said with a grin at Cora.

Cora laughed and climbed inside. We followed behind her as Elijah's playlist blasted from the car's speakers, mixing with everyone's rowdy chatter.

We arrived at school just as two white stretch limousines full of kids from our class turned into the driveway. We followed behind them, and when we stepped out onto the pavement and joined the milling throng, our excitement soared. A photographer snapped photos as we entered the gym, and we stopped to pose, asking him to take a group shot of all of us. I then linked my arm through Jake's and snuggled close for a couple's pic. I'd already decided it would be my new social media profile image, and I could hardly wait to upload it.

The gym had been lavishly decorated, and we looked around in awe. Helium-filled gold and silver balloons floated overhead, with a mass of sparkling curly ribbon hanging from each one. Offset by glittering fairy lights draped across the ceiling and walls, the sensation was of a twinkling night sky. It was all so beautiful and added to the specialty of the occasion.

Although most boys wore pants or jeans with shoes or sneakers, their button-up shirts added a formal touch. Several others wore suits and ties, a few had added vests like Sai's, and one even wore a top hat.

Even though every boy was dressed nicely, it was the girls who stole the show. Some wore heels, and others wore flats, and the various dresses were a mix of colors, fabrics, and styles. I spotted Ronnie in the crowd, her apricot dress studded with tiny jewels that caught the overhead lights and shimmered.

"I was so worried she'd choose the same dress as mine," Alexa confided.

Alexa had previously shared the details of her shopping spree, and I'd cringed as she described Ronnie's sudden appearance. "Her dress is really pretty, but yours is way nicer," I told Alexa.

I meant every word. Alexa's dress was a more stunning style, and she was so beautiful in teal blue. I'd also heard Damon gushing over how pretty she looked. When he reached for her hand and led her onto the dance floor, I nudged Brie. "How cute are they!"

"So cute!" she agreed, ecstatic to see the pair together. Alexa had been through so much since arriving in our town, and it was wonderful to see her so happy.

"Come on, Brie." I grabbed her hand impulsively. "Let's dance!"

I beckoned for the others to join us, and soon our entire group was on the dance floor together. I noticed Holly smile at Mike through the crowd. He returned her smile with a wave and a smile of his own. Reminded of my twin, a twinge of sympathy pricked at my skin. But when Jake reached for my hand and spun me in a circle, my focus shifted to the boy at my side.

When the song ended, and a slow song began, many people drifted to the perimeter of the dance floor. After a couple of dance sessions at school a few weeks earlier, we'd prepared for the slow dances. It was everyone's chance to pair up with their crush, and several girls waited to be asked, hopefully by the boy they liked.

Jake tugged on my hand and pulled me to him as we swayed back and forth. The dance steps we'd been taught were forgotten, but we didn't care. The romantic atmosphere added to the sight of Jake's beautiful face only inches from mine, and my heart fluttered with the wonder of it all.

Leaning in close, he whispered in my ear. "Have I told

you how beautiful you look?"

I nodded my head, my insides tumbling over at his words. "Yes, you have."

"Just making sure," he murmured, his sparkling eyes holding mine.

A shiver of joy, elation, and feelings I couldn't even describe rolled down my spine. I felt like the luckiest girl alive.

When I looked over Jake's shoulder and saw Alexa and Damon together, my happiness welled for my friend. Cora and Elijah had paired up too. They were also meant for each other. My gaze then shifted to Sai, who'd asked Lucy to dance. The pair laughed as they practiced the dance steps we'd learned in class. Brie also giggled madly as Jonah spun her around and around. I was so pleased to see everyone having fun. If only Ali were a part of it, the night would be perfect.

When I spotted Ronnie slide past with Brock, one of the good-looking boys from the football team, I wondered if he'd asked Ronnie to dance or if she had asked him. Most kids had paired up with someone, and although several remained with their friends at the edge of the dance floor, many had found a partner to enjoy the slow songs with.

I took particular notice of Mike's hand attached to Holly's waist. Ali had griped about the pair becoming closer, while I'd assured her that Mike was only interested in Holly as a friend. I now wondered if there was truth to my sister's musings. Deciding not to dwell on the issue, I returned my focus to Jake, soaking in the warmth of his arms around me. My eyes didn't stray again, and when another slow song began to play, I reveled in the thrill of the moment. It was simply too special for words.

When the music changed to a faster beat, Jake and I released our grip and danced our hearts out. At the end of the song, I stopped to catch my breath. It was a ton of fun, and I didn't want the night ever to end.

When Jake suggested we take a break, I arranged to

meet him in the foyer. He diverted to the refreshments stand by the far wall to get sodas for each of us while I made my way to the bathroom. Choosing a cubicle at the end of the row, I closed the door behind me.

A few seconds later, I heard Holly's voice as she entered the room. "Seriously, Ronnie, I think I'm in love."

My breath caught, and I stood silently listening. The unexpected conversation had caught me by surprise, and it seemed that Ali's fears had come to fruition.

"You two are perfect for each other!" Ronnie exclaimed. "He likes you, I can tell."

"I get the feeling that he does, but I'm still not sure."

"Of course, he does," Ronnie countered. "It's so obvious."

"He's so shy, though. He'll probably never do anything about it."

"Then it's up to you to let him know you like him. Tonight's the ideal opportunity."

"How am I supposed to do that?"

"I don't know," Ronnie giggled. "You'll figure something out. But meanwhile, I want a photo of you two together. I want to post it to Instagram, so Ali sees it. It's the ultimate revenge after what she did to us. I still can't believe she's not here. Hilarious. Suffer, Ali Jackson!" Ronnie chortled.

I gritted my teeth and resisted the urge to confront the pair. If Holly liked Mike, so be it, but why taunt Ali? She'd already been punished. It just wasn't necessary. I knew Jake would be wondering where I was, but I needed to hear the rest of the girls' conversation. I stilled my breathing and listened closely.

"I can be like Meg. She was all over him at the fundraiser disco," Holly giggled. "I was stuck at home, watching everyone's Instagram stories. It was the absolute worst. And when you posted the video of Meg and Mike together, I was fuming. If Ali sees me dancing with Mike, she'll probably feel the same way I did. It's so weird how our situations have reversed."

"It's her karma for what she did," Ronnie insisted. "Anyway, the more you're with Mike, the more attached he'll get. I mean, how could he refuse you? You look incredible tonight. I know he thinks so too. I've seen him watching you."

"Really? That makes me so happy."

I heard two cubicle doors open and close as the voices continued. Taking advantage, I quietly pushed my cubicle door open, quickly washed my hands, and scooted into the corridor. With my heart pounding, I joined Jake in the foyer. He smiled and passed me a soda which I sipped gratefully.

Ali was already distraught. I'd avoided adding anything to my Instagram story for fear of upsetting her further. I knew she'd be stalking everyone's social media accounts in the same way Holly had done, and I didn't want to add to my sister's pain. Ronnie was now ready to make everything much worse, and there was nothing I could do about it.

Hopefully, though, the scenario would encourage Ali to move on from Mike once and for all. Perhaps then, she'd finally fall for Sai. Brie, Alexa, and I all believed he was a much better choice anyway.

When Jake and I made our way back inside the gym, I happened to notice a couple huddled in a darkened corner. The glittery fabric of Lucy's white dress caught my eye, and when I realized Sai stood alongside her, I couldn't help staring. Sai's eyes were locked intensely on Lucy's as she spoke. When he brushed a loose strand of hair from her face, I frowned. Somehow, the gesture was too personal for a pair who were just friends. But then he leaned across and kissed her cheek.

I gasped aloud. Lucy was so reserved and quiet. The scene seemed totally out of character. And Sai was supposed to be obsessed with Ali. Or so I had thought. Had Sai and Lucy suddenly fallen for each other out of the blue? Or was it a crush that had developed over the past weeks, and I hadn't even noticed? Whatever the case, the revelation sent me reeling.

Ronnie was pushing Holly to be with Mike. Ronnie had tried with Meg and failed. She now saw this new scenario as the ultimate revenge against Ali. In the midst of all this, Lucy and Sai had somehow become an item as well, leaving Ali with no one.

While Ali didn't need to have a boy in her life, it seemed that every girl in our gang had paired up with someone. Everyone except my sister. We had the summer months ahead, and by the time Ali was finally ungrounded, the crushes would have developed even further.

With all the Instagram stories floating around as well as the gossip sure to circulate, Ali would soon figure out that detail. She was already depressed. The realization that everyone had moved on without her would throw her into even deeper despair. I'd experienced Ali's mood swings in the past, and if things snowballed the way I suspected they would, Ali's reaction wouldn't be pretty.

Jake grabbed my hand and tugged me back onto the dance floor. I tried to refocus and join in the fun, but my thoughts remained on my twin.

***

Find out what happens next!

Girl Gang – Book 2: The New Arrival is available Now!

If you enjoyed this book and have time to leave a review, it would be greatly appreciated.

Thanks once again for your support!
Katrina x

Please subscribe to our website katrinakahler.com
Or Follow us on Instagram @katrinakahler to stay up to
date with all our new releases.

BE SURE TO CHECK OUT
OUR OTHER BEST SELLING SERIES.

KIDS LOVE OUR BOOKS!